TWO BROTHERS

A STORY OF THE CIVIL WAR
AND BROTHERLY LOVE

By Robert J. Gossett

authorHOUSE®

AuthorHouse™
1663 Liberty Drive
Bloomington, IN 47403
www.authorhouse.com
Phone: 1-800-839-8640

Durham County Council Libraries, Learning and Culture	
C0 2 71 32097 F1	
Askews & Holts	
AF	

© 2012 Robert J. Gossett. All rights reserved.

No part of this book may be reproduced, stored in a retrieval system, or transmitted by any means without the written permission of the author.

Published by AuthorHouse 8/15/2012

ISBN: 978-1-4772-2560-8 (sc)
ISBN: 978-1-4772-2559-2 (hc)
ISBN: 978-1-4772-2561-5 (e)

Library of Congress Control Number: 2012911428

Any people depicted in stock imagery provided by Thinkstock are models, and such images are being used for illustrative purposes only. Certain stock imagery © Thinkstock.

This book is printed on acid-free paper.

Because of the dynamic nature of the Internet, any web addresses or links contained in this book may have changed since publication and may no longer be valid. The views expressed in this work are solely those of the author and do not necessarily reflect the views of the publisher, and the publisher hereby disclaims any responsibility for them.

This book is dedicated to the late Shirley Ranker,
who encouraged me to resume writing.

It is also dedicated to Tyler and Austin Seidman

and

Bob and John Gossett.

I wrote this for you guys. Please keep the spirit of brotherly love alive.

The author gratefully acknowledges the following people who assisted in this work:

Amy Slanchik, for being a superb typist and reader of my poor penmanship.

Sharon Slanchik, for being an expert editor.

John Slanchik, for his computer assistance.

Dennis Ray, for his expertise in proofreading.

Tih Kobolson, for her beautiful illustrations.

Table of Contents

CHAPTER 1	Ante Bellum, Texas	1
CHAPTER 2	The Winds of War Are Blowing	7
CHAPTER 3	On the Home Front	9
CHAPTER 4	Tragedy in the Family	11
CHAPTER 5	The Decline of Jeremy	17
CHAPTER 6	A New Face on the Farm	21
CHAPTER 7	Jeremy's Funeral	25
CHAPTER 8	Jimmy Sells the Farm	31
CHAPTER 9	Jimmy Becomes a Reporter	35
CHAPTER 10	Jimmy Reports on the War	39
CHAPTER 11	War in Galveston	47
CHAPTER 12	Back in Austin	51
CHAPTER 13	The Battle of Sabine Pass	55
CHAPTER 14	Jimmy and the Smugglers	59
CHAPTER 15	A Letter from Billy and a Note from Colleen	67
CHAPTER 16	The Investigation into the Syndicate Begins	71
CHAPTER 17	The Investigation Takes a Respite	81
CHAPTER 18	The Meeting	87
CHAPTER 19	The Golden Quill Awards	95
CHAPTER 20	Jimmy Takes on a New Assignment	97
CHAPTER 21	The Profiteers Go on Trial	107
CHAPTER 22	Jimmy and Colleen Are Married	121

Chapter 1

ANTE BELLUM, TEXAS

Jeremy and Cathy Dickens lived on a small farm not far from New Braunfels, Texas. Their home, a two-room log cabin, was built by the two of them from trees cut down when they cleared the land for farming. Their house may not have looked lavish to other people, but it was like a castle to them. They had been living in their Conestoga wagon until the house was completed. Counting the time they spent living in the wagon during their journey from Kentucky, it had been their home for almost a year.

The Dickens' were of Scotch Irish decent, while most of their neighbors were descendents of German immigrants. Despite their different backgrounds, they found their neighbors to be friendly and helpful, and when it came time for a housewarming and barn raising, more people showed up than were needed.

Their next-door neighbors, the Vogel's, quickly became their best friends. After the land was cleared and plowed, they planted corn, pole beans, potatoes, tomatoes, turnips, and beets. The land was a little bit hilly, but perfectly suitable for farming.

Jeremy dug a shallow well which produced limestone water, but perfectly suitable for drinking.

Their livestock consisted of two milk cows, two mules, a riding horse, four pigs, and a flock of chickens.

Their first crop came in about the same time Cathy delivered their first child, a boy, whom they named Billy.

Miss Braun delivered the baby. She bragged about the birth, saying, "This is the twenty-fifth baby I have delivered."

Miss Braun was a very large woman who probably weighed close to 300 pounds. Jeremy would watch when she got into her buggy as the springs seemed to collapse and the wheels sank into loose earth. He wondered how the one horse managed to pull the buggy.

After the delivery, Jeremy offered to pay her in cash but she refused, telling him, "No money. I have plenty; pay me with food. If you haven't noticed, I love to eat."

Jeremy filled a bushel basket with corn, tomatoes, and potatoes, loaded it into the buggy, and Miss Braun left for her home in town.

The farm did well, making them rich by no means, but supported them easily. Jeremy was not used to the warmer climate allowing two plantings a year, instead of the one they got in Kentucky.

Every Friday, Jeremy would load the wagon with produce and drive into town to sell at the farmer's market. He would usually buy an *Austin American Statesman* newspaper to keep up with the news.

Four years later, Miss Braun again visited the farm to deliver another boy they named Jimmy.

Billy was more excited than his parents as he dreamed of having a brother to play with. When Jimmy was a few weeks old, Billy would sit in the rocker holding him for as long as his mother would allow.

Cathy made sure she gave the same amount of attention and love to Billy as she did to baby Jimmy so as to not create jealousy between the two boys. The deep bonding and love of the boys for each other would later prove fruitful. As the boys grew older, this bond grew even stronger. Billy had appointed himself "Big brother guardian and protector of Jimmy." When the neighbor boy Hans came over to play, Billy would make sure Jimmy was not injured by the older boy's rough play.

Hans was Billy's age, but shorter than and not nearly as strong as him. When they wrestled, Billy was always able to pin him down easily.

Cathy and Jeremy were amazed at how quickly the time passed. Soon, Billy was a teenager and able to help Jeremy with the farm chores. He especially enjoyed the Friday trips to town for market day. This was the only day of the week he was able to get out of the home-schooling his mother provided.

Jeremy was getting disturbed by the talk at the market and the disagreement between those farmers who owned slaves and those who did not. At first he dismissed it as jealousy because some of them were rich enough to own slaves. He would later learn it was a moral issue. Some people did not believe a person had a right to take away a human's rights by enslaving them. It was an issue that would be decided later in a bloody war.

During one of his trips to market day, Billy met a young black boy named Rastus. "What's your last name?" Billy asked.

"Ain't got none. Slaves ain't 'lowed to have last names," was the reply.

Billy took a liking to Rastus, whose broad smile was contagious. He would tell his dad on the way home, "I wish that boy Rastus lived closer to us so we could play together."

"Son, he is a slave, and I'm afraid he wouldn't have time to play. He has to work in the fields just like his ma and pa," Jeremy answered him.

"But Dad, if he has to work so hard and never gets to play, how can he be so happy and smile all the time?" Billy asked.

"Well, son, some people are just in a good humor all of the time, regardless of how much adversity they face. He is just lucky his owner doesn't beat him for being so happy," Jeremy answered.

Over the next several years, during their trips to market day, the friendship grew between Billy and Rastus. Billy looked forward to talking and laughing with Rastus.

Jimmy was now twelve years old and able to go to market day with Billy and his dad. Jimmy looked forward to the trip to meet Rastus. Billy had told him so much about Rastus and his smile that Jimmy was curious to see what the black boy looked like.

When they reached their assigned stall at the market, Billy looked everywhere for Rastus, but he was nowhere to be found. They were puzzled. After the wagon was unloaded, Billy asked his dad to ask about Rastus. His dad checked with Rastus' owner, and returned to tell the boys the bad news, "Rastus is gone. His owner sold him. He said he got tired of looking at that stupid smile all the time," Jeremy informed them.

Billy argued, "But Dad, how could he do that? How could he just sell someone?"

Jeremy tried to explain, "The people who have slaves think they own them and they buy and sell them just like they do horses or cows. I personally don't believe in that, but if other people do, that is their business. It's not my place to judge them or tell them what to do. That's what they are all arguing about up in Austin right now. A man named Abraham Lincoln was just elected President of the United States. He doesn't believe in owning slaves, and he has said he is going to make it illegal to own them."

"But Dad, what will happen if he does that?" Jimmy asked.

"I really don't know, boys, but there is a lot of talk in Austin about not belonging to the United States anymore if that does happen. We'll buy a newspaper on the way home and see what is happening now up in Austin," Jeremy told the boys.

Buy a paper they did, and when they got home Jeremy read parts of the contents to his wife and two boys.

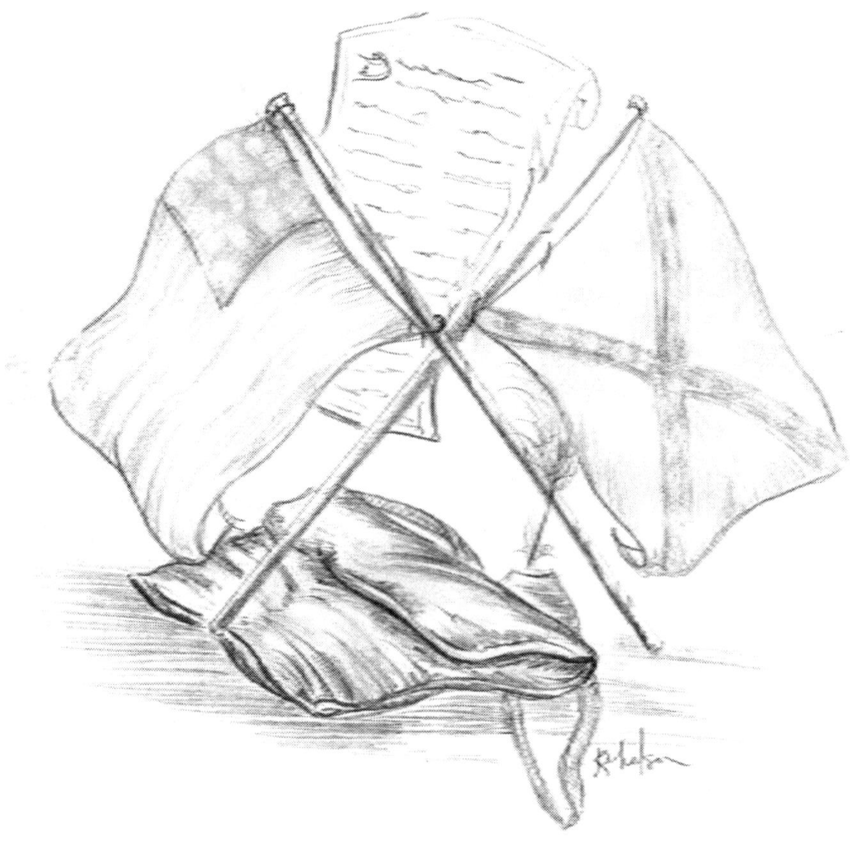

Chapter 2

THE WINDS OF WAR ARE BLOWING

The headline of the paper read: "To Secede or Not to Secede."

The article began, "County delegates met in Austin and voted to secede 66-8. Next step—Legislature will meet in February to vote on ratification."

"Uh oh," Jeremy added. "This most likely means Texas will secede and join the Southern Confederacy. We will most certainly be at war in a matter of months."

"Oh dear, what will that mean for the boys?" Cathy asked.

"Well, if we secede and join the Confederacy, I'm afraid Billy will be conscripted into the Southern Army when he turns eighteen next year," Jeremy reported.

Billy spoke up, "I'm not going to wait and be drafted; I'll just go ahead and enlist this year so I can pick out my own unit to serve in."

Cathy gasped, and Jeremy tried to console her saying, "Let's not all get our bowels in an uproar just yet. I'll keep buying the paper and see how this all plays out."

The debate in Austin continued. Some notable men were initially against secession, but putting their love of Texas ahead of their personal feelings, later relented.

Sam Houston was initially against secession, but changed his mind and voted for secession, but not for joining the Southern Confederacy. He wanted Texas to become an independent nation, as it had been after gaining its independence from Mexico.

James Weber Throckmorton originally voted against secession, but reversed his decision. He would rise to the rank of Brigadier General in the Confederate Army.

Things were happening so fast in Texas; Jeremy would make several trips to town solely to buy a newspaper to keep abreast of how the news might affect his family.

The family's worst fears were realized when on February 1, the legislature met and voted 166 to 8 to secede. This was the second largest margin for secession of any Confederate state. South Carolina had voted unanimously to secede. Not wanting to wait to be drafted, Billy started asking questions as to which options were open to him.

Terry's Texas Rangers was one regiment. These men would later furnish many men for the establishment of the Texas Rangers, a peacekeeping force in the old West.

Hoods' Texas Regiment was unified with infantry from Georgia, South Carolina, and Arkansas.

Walkers Grey Hounds was an all-Texas regiment, which included veterans of the Mexican American War and the Texas Revolution.

Billy was sworn in as a member of Hoods' Texas Regiment and ordered to report for duty in Austin, where he would get his uniform and equipment; he had to furnish his own horse and rifle. He already owned a horse, which he purchased from his share of the crops they sold at the market. For a rifle, Jeremy gave him a Kentucky long rifle given to him by his father. It had originally been a flintlock, but Jeremy had it converted to percussion cap when that technology became available.

Billy had persuaded his friend Hans to enlist with him. His parents violently objected but later relented. They had originally planned to move to Mexico with a group of their friends.

After hugs and kisses, Billy and Hans rode off together. Cathy was openly weeping and Jeremy had tears in his eyes, as did Jimmy. They stood and watched until the boys disappeared from sight. Jimmy secretly wished he had been able to go with them.

Chapter 3

ON THE HOME FRONT

Cathy knew she was three months pregnant when Billy rode off to war. But she and Jeremy did not tell him for fear it would add to his worries.

Jeremy continued to buy a newspaper as often as he could. He needed to stay up on events that were happening every day.

Jimmy was amazed how newspapers could gather information and disseminate it so quickly.

One major happening from San Antonio was reported. The state government selected four prominent citizens to call on Union General Whiting in San Antonio and call for the surrender of all Union arms and stores in the San Antonio area. Not only did they convince the general to surrender his entire command and a cache of 10,000 rifled muskets stored at the Alamo, they convinced him to accept a commission of general in the Confederate Army. This brought cries of "treason" from Unionists in the state.

Many families of Germans prepared to move to Mexico rather than live under Confederate rule. They left behind everything they could not load into wagons. Several entire villages made this trip and many were successful in relocating there.

One small band, however, was not as fortunate. As they neared the Nueces River, they were ambushed by a group of vigilantes and were massacred.

It was almost three weeks before the Dickens' got their first letter from Billy. He said he had completed his training and was on the way to Virginia with his regiment. He gave them an address to write him but said he would write later to give them another address. Cathy hurried to answer his letter but was afraid it would not reach him because the regiment was on the move.

Miss Braun paid a routine visit to check on Cathy, who was now seven months pregnant. She was concerned because Cathy was not gaining as much weight as she should have. After examining Cathy, Miss Braun rode off telling them she would be back next month.

Jeremy and Jimmy worked on the farm from daylight till dark, but still were getting behind in chores. They sure missed Billy, not only as a son and brother, but also as a farm hand. They still had crops to take to the market on Fridays, but the quantities were less and so was their income.

They watched for the mail rider, but so far had no further word from Billy. There had been no answer to Cathy's letter, and she began to worry, as any mother would.

When Miss Braun came for her monthly visit with Cathy, she found her in bed, unable get up. Jeremy and Jimmy did not realize she was bed bound because they both left before dawn to plow the south field.

From the field, they saw Miss Braun arriving in the carriage, enter the house, then rush out and hurriedly drive away.

Chapter 4

TRAGEDY IN THE FAMILY

Seeing Miss Braun depart in such a hurry, Jeremy and Jimmy rushed back to the house where they found Cathy in bed. She was sweating profusely and was having trouble breathing normally. They wished Miss Braun had stayed to help them as they tried to make Cathy as comfortable as possible, mopping her brow.

Within the hour, Miss Braun returned with Dr. Mason. Dr. Mason ran Jeremy and Jimmy out of the room, telling them to put on a fresh pot of coffee.

It was over an hour later when the doctor emerged, looking grim with terrible news for Jeremy.

"Jeremy, I'm sorry but I lost her."

"What was wrong? What happened?" Jeremy asked, shocked.

"The baby she was carrying died inside her, and I was unable to get it out before she succumbed. I'm sorry, but I did the best I could—I just didn't get here in time," he told them.

Jimmy instantly began crying, and Jeremy's eyes welled up. He was not far from crying himself.

"Was it a boy or a girl?" Jeremy asked.

"It was a little girl, and your wife's last request was to name her Sarah and bury her in the same grave as her," Dr. Mason told them.

Miss Braun finally finished cleaning up and joined them in the kitchen.

She said, "Jeremy, I am so sorry. If there is anything I can do, please let me know, and I will be happy to do it."

Jeremy replied, "There is one thing. If you know a preacher, please see if he could come and talk with me to arrange a funeral."

"I do know a Baptist minister, and I will have him come and see you," she said.

Dr. Mason then volunteered, "Jeremy, if you like, I can talk to the undertaker when I get back to town."

"That is very nice of both of you. Thank you both very much."

Miss Braun and the doctor left, leaving Jeremy and Jimmy to grieve privately. Jeremy instantly penned a letter to Billy telling him of his mother's death. He also wrote a letter to the Major he had met when Billy enlisted. He told the Major he had not heard from Billy and asked him to advise Billy, if he could, about his mother's death. He also inquired about the safety of his son.

He sent both letters to the last address he knew of, the address on the one letter he received from Billy.

The funeral at the Antioch Baptist church was a small one. So many people had moved away, were in the Army, or had simply lost their faith because of the war; all parishes had shrunk in size. Apparently Miss Braun had given the preacher some notes, because he delivered a beautiful eulogy, naming many of Cathy's qualities. Cathy was buried in the small cemetery next to the church. Her unborn daughter was buried in the casket with her, as was her last request.

Back at the farm, Jeremy and Jimmy resumed their chores, hoping staying busy would lessen their grief. Several of their neighbors brought food for them. Jimmy noticed a change in his father's manner. Jeremy smiled less, talked less, spent more time by himself, and hugged him more often. Jimmy noticed he took much more of an interest in news of the war.

When time permitted, they would ride into town, eat at the diner, and always buy a newspaper. Jeremy would read the paper and tell Jimmy if there was any news about the war.

One evening, Jimmy asked his dad, "How do they get that information so fast to get it in the newspaper so quickly?"

Jeremy explained, "Well son, they have reporters who follow armies around and telegraph stories to the newspaper, then they have people work all night to get the stories into the morning paper."

"Wow, Dad! That would be a really nice job."

Kidding him, Jeremy said, "You mean staying up all night to print the paper?"

"No, I mean being a reporter and getting stories to send in," he answered.

"Son, I know that sounds exciting, but you will probably be a farmer, just like me, and just like my daddy was," Jeremy told him.

Jimmy thought, *Maybe I won't be a farmer,* but said nothing.

About three weeks later the mail rider arrived with two letters for Jeremy. Not used to getting any mail, Jeremy ripped open both envelopes and read them. One letter was from Billy:

> Dear Dad and Jimmy,
> Sorry I didn't write sooner but we have been marching so fast, and I get so tired that I just eat and go to sleep. They sure are in a hurry to get somewhere, but they won't tell us where. Some men say we're still going to Virginia, but they don't really know.
> I'm so sorry Mom died. I know it must be hard for you and Jimmy; I wish I could be there to help. Will write again when I can.
> --Billy

Jeremy carefully folded the letter and put it in his shirt pocket. Then he read the next letter. It was written on stationary marked "C.S.A." It read:

> Dear Mr. Dickens,
> Thank you for your inquiry into your son William's status.
> I am pleased to report your son is alive and well. He has performed very well and has exhibited leadership skills which resulted to his being promoted to Corporal. My condolences on the death of your wife. I have passed the information on to William. I am sure you will be hearing from him soon. Major Bunnels also sends his condolences.
> Walter C. Smith—1st Lt. Adjutant
2nd Texas Regiment
Confederate States Army

Jeremy also folded this letter and put it into his pocket with the other one. He then remarked to Jimmy, "That is no coincidence that both letters came at the same time. That lieutenant probably ordered Billy to write it."

"Probably, but at least we heard from him," Jimmy agreed.

From the tone of Billy's letter, Jeremy expected something major would be happening in Virginia in the near future. He was now buying a paper almost every day and scanning it very carefully. He and Jimmy found a new restaurant in town where they could order bacon or ham and eggs with biscuits for ten cents. Coffee or milk was an additional five cents, so usually they would just drink water. Jeremy calculated that if they had this cheap breakfast and got a sandwich for lunch, they only had to cook one meal a day—supper. This usually consisted of beans or potatoes with ham and biscuits. After a hard day in the fields, neither of them felt like doing much cooking.

Another month passed before the big event Jeremy had been expecting finally appeared in the morning paper, dated September 19, 1862:

> Bloody Battle at Sharpsburg, Virginia
>
> A total of 500 cannons traded fire as Confederate troops battled for 12 continuous hours in the 70-degree weather. At dawn Confederate troops emerged from the fog and began attacking the Union soldiers' encampment.
>
> Wave after wave of Confederate soldiers advanced toward the Union Army but was driven back by cannon and musket fire.
>
> Likewise Union troops counterattacked and were repelled for almost 12 hours before the Confederate forces were forced to withdraw.
>
> Some of the Union success was due to a lot of Union troops armed with the new rapid fire Henry rifle. It was a 16-shot lever action-repeating rifle, far superior to the single shot muzzle-loading rifles used by the rebel troops. The Confederates called it "That damned Yankee rifle they could load on Sunday and fire all week."
>
> A total of 13,000 Confederate troops were killed, wounded, captured or deserted. The Union troops fared

a little better with 10,000 killed or wounded. They had no desertions.

Jeremy's eyes began to fill with tears as he read and re-read the article. Over and over he repeated, "I knew it. I just knew it. That's where his unit was headed when he said they were going to Virginia."

"Now Dad, we don't really know that, and we can hope and pray he wasn't one of the casualties," Jimmy told him, trying to console him.

"Well, I'm going to write him another letter right now and see if we get an answer," Jeremy said.

He did write the letter, and Jimmy gave it to the mail rider the next morning.

During the night, through the thin wall between their bedrooms, Jimmy heard his dad sobbing loudly. Jimmy thought, *That newspaper article has convinced Dad that Billy was killed or wounded.*

Jimmy was up early the next morning. He was hungry. He and his dad didn't have supper the night before because of the excitement caused by the newspaper article. The cows needed milking. The chickens had to be fed, and the hogs slopped. Jimmy would take care of these chores before he had breakfast. He hayed the livestock, fed the chickens, milked the cow, and gathered the eggs, and then he went into the house and made a pot of coffee. Then before eating, he tried to get his dad up but got the response, "Son, I'm not ready to get up yet. You go ahead and go to town and eat, but don't forget to bring me a paper."

Chapter 5

THE DECLINE OF JEREMY

Jimmy was only 15, but he was old enough to understand something was wrong with his dad. He did ride into town, ate, got a paper, but then not knowing who else to talk to, he went to see Miss Braun.

When she opened the door to him, he told her, "I'm sorry to bother you, but I don't know who else to ask for help."

"You poor child, come in here; sit down and tell me what is wrong," she said. He told her of the article in the paper and his dad's response—how he had cried himself to sleep and didn't want to get out of bed this morning.

"Oh my, no doubt he is still grieving over your mother, and now thinking your brother is hurt or killed—it might be too much for him to bear. Tell you what I'll do; I'll pay a social visit on you this afternoon and see if he will talk to me," she said.

"Thank you, Miss Braun. I'm sorry to be a bother to you. See you this afternoon," Jimmy said.

Feeling relieved, he rode home and found his dad still in bed. Again he tried to get him up, but his dad refused.

True to her word, Miss Braun visited the house that afternoon. Jimmy noticed that she now had two horses pulling her buggy instead of one.

I wonder if she gained more weight, he thought.

The always-cheerful Miss Braun came into the house, and Jimmy invited her to sit on the sofa. Then he called to his dad.

"Hey Dad, Miss Braun is here to pay us a visit," he yelled.

"Tell her to go away. I don't feel like talking today," came the response.

Jimmy looked at Miss Braun, who said nothing but motioned for him to follow her outside.

Out of earshot of Jeremy, she told him, "Son, I am worried about him. Let's wait a few more days, and if he isn't better, we will have to try something else. Maybe he will get up when he gets hungry enough."

"Thank you, Miss Braun. You are really a nice person to help me," he told her.

"No thanks needed, my boy. I'll be back in a few days," she told him as she drove off.

Jeremy got up the second day, but still did not feel like working. He was able to cook breakfast for the two of them and drink some coffee. Jimmy did the chores and was glad to see his dad out of bed and feeling better.

The third day Jeremy announced, "Son, I'm sure you will be OK staying here alone for a few days. I'm going to ride up to Austin and see if I can find out something about Billy."

"Sure, Dad. I'll be fine. I'd like to know something too," Jimmy answered.

Jeremy saddled his horse and rode away. While he was gone, Miss Braun came by. Jimmy explained where his dad had gone, and Miss Braun responded, "Good. It might be a good sign he is feeling well enough to make that trip. Will you be OK?"

"I'll be fine. I have plenty of work around here to keep me busy," Jimmy replied.

"Well, you be careful, and let me know if I can do anything for you," she said.

Jimmy busied himself with hard work the next two days, and then his dad arrived.

"What news do you have?" Jimmy asked him.

His dad replied, "I really didn't learn anything about Billy. His name wasn't on any of the casualty lists, but they told me the lists were not complete. I did find Hans Vogel's name though, and he has been wounded and captured. Let's not say anything to the Vogels though. It might only worry them."

"OK, Dad. Now come inside, and I'll fix us some supper."

"Sounds good, son. I am hungry."

Jimmy thought, *That is a good sign; maybe he is getting better.*

But he wasn't getting better. After dinner he again reread the article about the battle and had no energy for anything else.

The next morning Jeremy slept late while Jimmy busied himself with the chores. He was able to keep up with the everyday tasks, but the north field needed plowing to plant a new crop of corn, and he had no time to do it.

That night he told his dad, "Dad, I just can't keep up with everything around here. The north field needs plowing so we can plant corn, and I just don't have time to do it."

"Just do the best you can," was the answer.

The next morning was Friday, so Jimmy loaded the wagon and got ready to go to the market.

He told his dad, "I'm going in to the market. Want to go with me?"

"No son, you go ahead. Just remember to bring me a newspaper."

As he rode off he thought, *Why do I have to do all this work alone? Dad is strong enough to help me; he just won't do it.*

Jimmy was becoming irritated by his dad's actions, or rather, lack of actions. He wished he knew what to do.

He returned home that evening with less money than they ordinarily received because their crops were dwindling and had not been replanted.

As soon as he went into the house, he realized he had forgotten the newspaper. It didn't really matter because Jeremy was asleep and wouldn't wake up until the next morning.

When he did wake up, Jimmy fixed him some eggs, ham, and biscuits and he ate it in bed. He only ate about half of it, then went back to sleep.

That afternoon Miss Braun came by to check on Jeremy. When Jimmy told her what was going on she said, "I'm going to send Dr. Mason out here to give your dad a checkup. Will you be home?"

"Yes, ma'am. I don't go any place except to market on Friday," he answered her.

Dr. Mason arrived as Jimmy was milking the cows. "Hello, Jimmy. How's your dad this morning?"

"I don't know, sir. He was still sleeping when I started my chores," he replied.

After examining Jeremy, the doctor came outside to talk to Jimmy, "Well, son, there is nothing physically wrong with your dad. He told me he didn't have anything to live for, and that he just wants to die. And I'm afraid if he doesn't start eating more and sleeping less, he will do that."

Jimmy told him, "I fix him food, but he only eats a little bit of it."

"Are you trying to do everything around here by yourself?"

"Yes, sir. I don't have anyone to help me."

"Well, I just happen to know someone who might be able to help. There is an Irish family on a farm not far from here. They have eight boys and two girls, and there isn't enough work on their small farm to keep them all busy. One of the girls is sixteen and a hard worker. If you could afford to pay her 50 cents a day, I'm sure she would be glad to work for you. Her name is Colleen Sweeney."

"I could probably pay her that for three or four days a week. Would that be OK?" Jeremy asked.

"I'm sure that would be fine. I'll send her out in the morning," Dr. Mason said.

"Thank you, sir. You have been a big help."

"Just doing my job. And don't fret over your daddy too much. If he wants to live, he will, and if he wants to die, he will do that as well. It's up to him, and there is nothing any of us can do," the doctor told him.

Jimmy fought back his tears as best he could.

Chapter 6

A NEW FACE ON THE FARM

The next morning Colleen Sweeney rode up on a beautiful Shetland pony.

She introduced herself and said, "Dr. Mason said I could work for you three days a week."

Jimmy studied her carefully. She had beautiful red hair, green eyes, and a fair complexion with freckles. Although only a year younger than Jimmy, she was six inches shorter. Her frame was skinny, and her hands were calloused from doing hard farm work.

"I'm a good cook, and I know how to do chores and am a good worker," she told him.

"I'm sure you will do fine. Can you come Mondays, Wednesdays, and Fridays? On Friday I have to take crops in to the market, and I hate to leave my dad here alone," Jimmy explained.

"Dr. Mason told me about your dad. Does he ever get out of bed?" she asked.

"Not very often, and when he does, it isn't for very long. When he does eat, he eats in bed, and then he barely finishes what I give him," he explained.

"Well, maybe he'll eat more if I feed him," she said.

Colleen Sweeney turned out to be a real jewel. She cooked two meals every day, kept the house as neat as a pin, and did a lot of the light chores at the farm.

Relieved of some of the chores, Jimmy was able to plow and plant a new crop. He was a month late in getting it done, but if the weather held he should get another crop to harvest before winter.

One day, Colleen was baking bread, and the wonderful aroma scented the entire house. Jeremy, upon smelling the aroma, yelled, "Cathy, is that you baking bread? Have you come back to me?"

"No, Mr. Dickens. It's only me baking bread," Colleen answered.

Jeremy collapsed back onto the bed.

Even with Colleen's help, Jimmy was not able to keep the crops planted, as they should be, even working from dawn to dark. He wondered how long he would be able to keep up the pace. It was Monday morning when Colleen came, fixed breakfast, and took a tray into feed Jeremy. She was not able to wake him, and no one would ever be able to wake him. He was dead.

Chapter 7

JEREMY'S FUNERAL

Jeremy's funeral was at the same church as Cathy's was held. He was buried next to Cathy in the church cemetery.

Jimmy noticed the same people were at this funeral as his mother's. He noticed that the Vogels, his neighbors, did not attend either of the funerals. In fact, he had not seen them since Billy and Hans went away to war.

Jimmy went home later and wrote a letter to Billy to advise him of their father's passing. He doubted he would hear anything because there was no return letter from him when Jeremy wrote him about the death of his mother. He wondered, *Was Billy dead, or wounded, or a prisoner in some horrible prison?*

That evening after dinner, Colleen sat on the sofa with Jimmy and surprised him when she asked, "Jimmy, will you marry me?"

"What kind of a question is that? You are only 16, and I am only 17 and too young to marry," Jimmy answered.

"Well, I just wondered. I have these terrible throbs, and mother said they would go away when I get married," she said.

"What kind of throbs? Where are they at?" he asked.

"They are down there between my legs. You know, in my place mother calls my valentine. My nasty brothers call it my pussy, but daddy slaps them when he hears it. I hate it because I have to touch it to make it stop, and sometimes when I get it to stop, I make sounds," she told him.

"What kind of sounds?" he asked, his curiosity aroused.

"Well you know, sometimes grunts, sometimes sighs, and sometimes screams," she announced.

"I never heard of that," he said.

"Well, it feels good when it stops but I sleep with my little sister, and I'm afraid she will hear me," she explained.

"Well, then if you won't marry me, will you make love to me and see if that will cure the throbbing?" she asked.

"Colleen, I'm ashamed of you, asking me that." Jimmy was feeling embarrassed.

"Well, then if you won't make love to me, next time I get to throbbing, will you touch me and see if it stops?"

"I don't know. I'll have to think about that. I'm not sure that would be right," he responded.

"OK, you think about it, and I'll let you know next time I get the throbs," she said as she left for home.

Jimmy had a tough time getting to sleep that night. He kept thinking about his parents, his brother, and Colleen's throbs. He wished she had never told him about that. Jimmy made sure he was busy working when Colleen rode up the next morning. He hitched the mule to the plow and was plowing a field along the road. It got a lot of sunshine, and he considered it a prime place to grow tomatoes.

He had the field half finished when he saw a pitiful sight. He spied a one-legged man trying to hobble down the road using a crutch, which had obviously been cut from a tree limb.

Fearing it might be Billy, he unhitched the mule, jumped on its back, and rode toward the crippled man. As he neared, he saw that it was not Billy. It was Hans.

"Hey, Hans, it's me, Jimmy!" he yelled.

"Hello, Jimmy. Can you help me get home?" he asked.

"Of course I will, Hans, but what happened to you?" he asked.

"I got a damned Yankee minnie ball in the leg. It got infected, and I got gangrene, and some Yankee doctor had to cut off my leg to save my life," he explained.

"Sure I will, Hans," he said as he helped Hans onto the mule and led him toward his house.

Hans commented, "I hate for Mama and Papa to see me like this, but at least I'm alive," he said.

"I'm sure they will be glad to see you. We haven't heard anything from Billy. Was he at Sharpsburg with you?" Jimmy asked.

"Yeah, he was there. In fact, he tried to help me after I got shot, but he had to leave before the Yanks caught him too," Hans related.

"So he was OK then, but do you know what happened to him later?"

"Yeah, I heard about him. There were so many deserters after the battle, the army asked for volunteers to go after them, and Billy volunteered. They were supposed to bring them back to face court martial for desertion under fire, or kill them if they resisted. What I heard was he brought more back dead, draped over their horses, than he brought back alive," Hans related.

"Holy shit," Jimmy responded.

By that time they were at the Vogel house. When his parents saw him, they both hugged him, almost knocking him off his one foot.

Then Mrs. Vogel saw Jimmy and told him, "Jimmy, you go home, and don't come back here. If it hadn't been for that damned evil brother of yours, my Hans wouldn't be in this condition."

Jimmy said, "I was just trying to help Hans."

Hans said, "Thanks, Jimmy. We'll talk some more later."

Jimmy left thinking, *I should have known she would blame Billy for poor Hans.*

Feeling too downhearted, he put away the mule and plow and went into the house, hoping Colleen would fix some lunch.

Colleen ate lunch with him, and he told her all about Hans and about what he learned about Billy's happenings. After lunch Jimmy sat on the sofa, and Colleen sat next to him.

She told him, "Oh, Jimmy, I have been throbbing so much this morning—will you touch me and make it stop?"

"Why the hell not? I haven't done anything right all day. Maybe this will make one of us feel better," he told her.

He reached under her dress and felt the bloomers, but she told him, "No, Jimmy, under the bloomers."

As soon as he started touching her, she began moaning and gyrating the lower part of her torso. After several minutes, she uttered a scream of delight and her body relaxed.

"Oh, Jimmy, that feels so much better. Next time, want me to touch you too?"

"We'll see," he replied.

For the next six months Jimmy continued to farm, take crops to the market, and touch Colleen when she asked for it. So far he hadn't asked her to touch him.

Jimmy was not really keeping up the farm as well as he felt he should have. And he was tired, bone tired; every day he wished he could get to be a newspaper reporter, a dream he had fostered for a long time.

One day after lunch the mail rider arrived and had a letter from Billy. Jimmy was surprised but anxiously ripped open the envelope and read:

> Dear Jimmy,
> Sorry I couldn't write before, but I travel all of the time looking for deserters.
> I was sorry we lost Mom and Dad. Sorry I am so long telling you. I will probably never be able to come home. I have made so many enemies, I am afraid I will be killed if they catch up with me. That's why I stay on the move.
> When I'm discharged from the Army, I am going out west, maybe to Colorado or California.
> Jimmy, about the farm, as far as I am concerned it is all yours. Farm it, sell it, or whatever. I will never farm again; I have found an easier way to make a living.
> I'll try and write again some time. You be good. I will always love you.
>
> Your brother,
> Billy

Jimmy was shocked and saddened that he might never see his brother again. He loved him, too.

He read the letter again, this time aloud so Colleen could hear it.

He was beginning to get tears in his eyes thinking he might never see his brother again. Colleen noticed and told him, "Jimmy, please don't cry. Everything will work out for you."

He replied, "It's this damned farm. I am tired of trying to work it all by myself. I think I'll just sell it."

"I wish you wouldn't talk like that, but if you are serious about selling it, I'll tell my daddy. He has been thinking about selling his place and buying a larger farm so he can support our big family better," Colleen told him.

"Sure, tell him. At least we can talk about it," he said.

The next morning, Colleen arrived with her daddy, John Sweeney.

John was nothing like Jimmy had pictured him to be. He stood a few inches under six feet, with a slight build except for an oversized belly. The hair he had left was red. His face was furrowed and tanned. He had piercing blue eyes that seemed to look right through whatever he was looking at.

He said to Jimmy, "Nice to meet you, son. Colleen has told me a lot about you, and she said you were thinking about selling this farm."

"Yes, sir. I have thought a lot about it. I just don't know what to ask for it," Jimmy responded.

"Well, I have been thinking about selling my place and getting a bigger one. Mind if I look around?"

"No sir. You go right ahead," Jimmy said.

John began walking completely around the perimeter of the farm, inspecting each field and picking up handfuls of dirt and examining it. After about an hour, he returned saying, "This is a nice farm, and I'm interested in it."

"How do we go about setting a price?" Jimmy asked.

"The only fair way is to have Mr. Ritter from the land office inspect both farms and set a price on both of them," John said.

"When will he do that?" Jimmy asked.

"I'll try and get him here this week. Are you going to be home all week?"

"Yes, sir, except on Friday when I go to the market," Jimmy told him.

"OK, then I'll be in touch," John told him and left for home.

When Friday arrived, Jimmy still hadn't heard from John. He loaded his crops to head for the market. He took every available crop, even eggs, which he had not sold before. He would need cash to look for work in town. Colleen did not work on Fridays, and Jimmy was feeling alone and depressed as he drove the wagon to town.

The ride home that evening was much more pleasant. He had sold all of his crops and eggs and had more money than he had ever had before. With more than $75 in his pocket, he celebrated by eating dinner at the German restaurant. With his stomach filled with sauerbraten, slaw, potato pancakes, and applesauce, he headed for home.

Chapter 8

JIMMY SELLS THE FARM

On Saturday morning, John Sweeney arrived with Bill Ritter from the land office. Ritter had already appraised the Sweeney farm and thought he had a buyer for it. He then spent over an hour appraising Jimmy's farm. The good news for everyone was Sweeney had enough cash to pay the difference in price between the two farms. Now all that remained was to sell the Sweeney place. This happened the next week, and suddenly Jimmy had nothing but an envelope full of cash. No farm, no house, only his saddle horse, clothes, and his dad's Colt revolver.

Things happened so quickly the next week he could barely believe what was happening. He put most of the proceeds from the farm in a bank account in his and Billy's name. He rented a room in Mrs. Willis' boarding house, answered an ad in the *Austin American Statesman* by telegraph, and was hired as a printer's devil. He didn't even know what a printer's devil was, but he needed a job, and he would be working for a newspaper. Knowing he would have to leave on Saturday for Austin, he spent Friday saying good-bye to Miss Braun, and then went to see his friends at market day. There he saw Colleen and her daddy and brothers, who brought their crops to the market.

Colleen whispered to him as she hugged him, "Tell me where you are staying, and I will come to see you tonight. I am throbbing really badly."

Women were not ordinarily allowed to visit the boarders, but Mrs. Willis knew Colleen from their church and put her blessing on the visit.

Jimmy told her of his job in Austin and promised to write her and send her his new address when he got settled.

Colleen visited Jimmy later that evening. She insisted on him touching her, and for the first time he agreed she could touch him at the same time. In a few minutes Colleen was grunting, and Jimmy began low-pitched grunts himself.

He told her, "You were right. It is much better when someone does the touching for you."

She laughed and kissed him saying, "Oh, Jimmy, I hate that you are leaving. Can I come to Austin and see you sometime?"

He answered, "Of course. I told you I will send you my address when I get settled."

Early Saturday morning Jimmy packed his few possessions in his saddlebags and rode off to a new adventure in Austin.

He reported for work early Monday morning, meeting Ed Harris, assistant print shop foreman.

Harris told him, "We don't ordinarily hire people sight unseen, but this damned war has drained off all of the available men in the area."

Harris took him to his work place, gave him a printer's apron, and put him to work. By the end of the day, he had learned what a printer's devil was. His main job was breaking down the type from the previous night's printing and sorting each letter of type into the appropriate compartment. He soon learned to do it quickly and with few errors. He knew if he made an error, he would catch hell from the typesetter, who was using the type to set up tomorrow's paper. He also had to do anything the typesetter asked him to do. After work he was tired, dirty, and somewhat bewildered, but happy. He was actually working for a newspaper. That evening, he wrote Billy telling him about the sale of the farm, the bank account in the New Braunfels bank, and his job at the *Austin American Statesman*. As he had promised he also wrote Colleen and gave her his new address.

Jimmy enjoyed his new room at the boarding house. It was clean, quiet, and inexpensive.

Mrs. Honeywell, whom everyone called Honey, was a large, jovial, friendly widow. She and her black lady helper served breakfast every morning and dinner every day but Sunday.

She had taken a liking to Jimmy and made him a lunch to take to work from the previous night's dinner leftovers. Jimmy worked six days a week and soon became very proficient in tearing down the newspaper pages. Every night he would take home the previous day's paper and he read every page. He was searching for news of the war and Billy in particular.

After four months on the job, Jimmy was promoted to typesetter and got a nice pay raise. He had earned the respect of Ed Harris, whom Jimmy suspected had gotten him the promotion. Harris had also been promoted to assistant editor.

After setting type for six months, Jimmy was summoned to Ed Harris' office. Fearing he had done something wrong, he was filled with apprehension. Harris greeted him with, "Jimmy, get your ass in here. I have something to ask you."

Chapter 9

JIMMY BECOMES A REPORTER

Now with even more apprehension, Jimmy entered the office.

Harris told him, "Jimmy, I know you are a good worker. How would you like to be a reporter?"

"I would love it. I have always dreamed of being a reporter," Jimmy answered.

"I think I should warn you, I have had two reporters killed covering the war. Does that scare you?" Harris asked.

"No, sir. I can take care of myself and get stories for you," Jimmy responded.

"OK, you're hired. I'll pay you $4 a day plus expenses and a $20 bonus for every usable story you send me. I'll give you a tip. Hang around bars and get tips, and then follow up on them. Send me a telegram at least once a week and let me know what you will be reporting on. If you get some good stories, wire them in. Now get going and do a good job. Get me some stories," Harris told him.

Jimmy had followed the war by carefully reading the newspaper. He knew that Union forces had landed in Brownsville in January and were rumored to be marching to Corpus Christi. So he packed his clothes in his saddlebags, told Mrs. Honeywell he would be gone for a while, and rode off for Corpus Christi.

The third day he arrived there and visited Romeo's Tequila Bar. Fortunately, Romeo spoke broken English, and when Jimmy flashed his brand new press credentials, he was told a small rag tag unit of Confederate soldiers, sheriff's deputies, cowboys, and ranch owners were riding out to meet Union soldiers marching to Corpus Christi.

Hearing that, he downed his beer, thanked Romeo, and rode south. He had traveled fast and caught up with the unit before sundown. Jimmy showed his press credentials again and was introduced to Colonel Ray Davis and his unit of soldiers, cowboys, ranchers, and volunteers. Jimmy was invited to follow the unit if he promised to fight when the unit was engaged. Jimmy had his Colt revolver, so he agreed. He camped with the men that night, and early the next morning a scout reported that a force of 500 regular Union soldiers was marching north about a half day's march away.

Colonel Davis wasted no time formulating a battle plan. He would split his men into two units, each hidden on either side of the trail. He instructed his troops to let half of the enemy unit pass by then open fire when he fired the first shot. The men finished breakfast, put out the fires, then concealed themselves on both sides of the trail. The unsuspecting Union troops marched four abreast led by a regular army captain, a bugler, and a standards bearer. Colonel Davis directed a group of mounted men to station themselves a quarter of a mile up the trail and charge when the bugler blew "Charge!"

Jimmy was becoming very nervous as he stood beside Colonel Davis awaiting the action.

He could only hope he would not shame himself. He had never shot at a human before. A hush fell over the rebel troops as they listened to the sounds of a marching enemy growing louder.

When the unsuspecting Union soldiers continued marching forward, Colonel Davis decided half had gone by, so he fired the first shot. Jimmy fired the second one. Then all hell broke loose. The unprepared enemy fell in huge numbers. A lot of the cowboys and ranchers owned Henry rifles, and all of the volunteers were using revolvers, so their rate of fire was three or four times that of the Union soldiers. After only a few minutes, most of the Union soldiers were on the ground, dead or wounded.

The first part of the Union detachment now returned to help their comrades. Then the rebel bugler sounded the charge and the twenty mounted rebels, screaming and shooting, drove them back into the deadly crossfire. Fearing his entire unit would be wiped out, the captain ordered a retreat. What was left of his unit, carrying some of their wounded soldiers, retreated to the south.

Colonel Davis screamed to his men, "Let them go. We have no way to handle prisoners."

After the half-hour battle was over, Jimmy counted over 200 bodies, and he guessed there were 50 wounded. The Union had lost over half of its force. The rebels had only eight dead and five wounded.

Jimmy was told by Colonel Davis, "Those Yanks might be good soldiers, but they don't know a damned thing about how the Indians fight. We do."

Later one of the ranchers told Jimmy, "Let me give you some advice that might help you live a little longer. Don't ever stand next to an officer during a battle. The enemy is trying to kill him first, and they might accidentally get you."

Jimmy thanked him for the advice, and rode back to Corpus Christi to file his report to the paper.

Jimmy was feeling queasy. He was horrified by the carnage. He had never seen so many dead and wounded people. One of the sights that upset him was the dead Union soldiers killed with their rifles still slung over their shoulders. He hoped if he had killed anyone it wasn't one of them. He felt like he might have to vomit, so he stayed to himself.

Chapter 10

JIMMY REPORTS ON THE WAR

In a wire to the paper he said:

> Southern forces and civilian volunteers routed over 500 Union soldiers 10 miles south of Corpus Christi.
> Though outnumbered 5 to 1, the rebels under the command of Colonel Ray Davis used Indian tactics to kill or wound over half of the Union troops marching against them. The rebels suffered minimal losses.
> Signed,
> Jimmy Dickens, Reporter
> Respond to Harbor Hotel, Corpus Christi

Jimmy checked into the hotel, got a bath, ate a light supper, and then slept like a baby. The next morning he found a return telegram waiting for him at the hotel desk. It read:

> Good work. Excellent job of reporting. Article will be lead story in tomorrow's paper. Now head toward Galveston. We have info Southern forces will try to retake city of Galveston.
> Signed,
> Ed Harris--Editor

While he had breakfast in the hotel coffee shop, he was feeling proud of himself. He thought, *A headline with my very first story.*

Then he sat and made careful entries in his expense journal. He was spending more money than he was used to spending, and he couldn't afford not to be reimbursed.

As he left town he bought a new box of cartridges for his Colt. He didn't remember how many shots he had fired, but he did remember having to reload four times, so he had shot between 24 and 30 times. He sure didn't want to be caught without enough ammunition. When he told the gun shop owner where he was headed, the owner advised him to avoid Port Lavaca.

He reported the Yankees had captured the town a year ago and checked on any traffic coming into town. Jimmy thanked him, rode all day, and finding no place to rent a room for the night, he camped out. For dinner he had beans and three-day old biscuits he brought with him. He fed his horse with a feedbag of oats he always carried in a saddlebag for just such an emergency. He spread his bedroll, built a small fire, and using his saddle for a pillow, he was soon asleep.

Up at daylight, he rolled up his bedroll, saddled his horse, and was on his way to Galveston, following the advice of a friendly farmer. By noon he was in Victoria and found a diner where he could eat his first meal of the day.

While eating lunch he saw another patron reading a copy of the *Austin American Statesman*. He asked to borrow the paper and read the headline: "SOUTHERN FORCES FOIL YANKEE INVASION OF CORPUS CHRISTI." Then he saw the byline: "Story by Jimmy Dickens." He was so proud of himself. He had a byline—unheard of for a cub reporter.

Pointing at the headline he told the reader of the paper, "Hey, that's mine."

"Like hell it is. I just bought this paper," the man responded.

Jimmy hastened to explain, "No, I don't mean the paper. That's my article. I'm Jimmy Dickens."

The man smiled, "Oh, I see. Good going, son."

Jimmy told the man that he was on the way to Galveston and asked for directions.

He was told to go northeast to Shiner, where he could spend the night, then be close to Galveston the following day.

Thanking the man, Jimmy replenished his supplies and rode off to Shiner.

In Shiner he found no hotel but only a boarding house, so he got a room there. He paid the owner's son 10 cents to care for his horse, then ate dinner and went to bed early.

Breakfast was served at six the next morning, and Jimmy was waiting to be served. While he drank coffee he talked to another boarder, who asked him what his occupation was.

"I am a reporter with the *Austin American Statesman*," Jimmy explained.

"Got any proof of that?" the man asked him.

Jimmy produced his press credentials.

"Sorry son, but those damned Yanks have spies scattered all over around here. I was just being careful," the man explained. Jimmy thought back to the man he met in Victoria, and wondered if he had been a spy. He would not reveal his destination to anyone else.

"Where you headed?" the man asked.

"Just going to Houston to see if I can dig up a story," he lied.

After a quick breakfast, Jimmy saddled his horse and rode off toward Galveston. Once he had to avoid a Yankee patrol. He could hear their equipment battling, so he made a wide swing around them.

It was beginning to get dark, and he knew he could never find Galveston in the dark.

He noticed a ranch house, so he decided to stop and ask directions. Passing through a gate, he noticed above the gate a hand-carved wooden sign saying, "WWW Ranch."

He rode to the house and knocked on the door. It was answered by a middle-aged man, with pistol in hand.

"Who are you and what might your business be?" he was asked.

Jimmy answered him, "Sorry to bother you, sir, but my name is Jimmy Dickens. I'm a reporter for the *Austin American Statesman*. I was on my way to Galveston and knew I couldn't find it after dark, so I decided to stop and ask directions."

"Got any proof of who you are?" the rancher asked.

Jimmy produced his credentials and was invited inside.

"Sorry to be so rude, but those damned Yanks have spies all over the place. I'm Walter Wheeler, and she is Wilma Wheeler," he said, pointing to his wife. Do you know what day this is?" Wheeler asked.

"No, sir, I don't. I know I left Austin on December 12th, and I've been traveling ever since."

Well, young man, it is Christmas Eve, and I'm sure not going to turn away anyone tonight. You make yourself at home. We have a spare bedroom, and you're welcome to spend the night," Wheeler told him.

Over a delicious dinner of brisket, beans, and fried potatoes with cornbread, they talked.

Jimmy explained he had just come from the battle of Corpus Christi.

"We haven't heard about that; what happened?" Walter said.

"Well, the Yanks marched towards Corpus Christi with about 500 men. They were no match for Colonel Davis' group of 100 men. They ambushed the Yanks Indian-style and massacred them. The Yanks lost over half of their men, and we only suffered minimum losses," Jimmy explained.

"Were you there?" Walter asked.

"Not only was I there, but I was part of it. Colonel Davis told me I had to fight if I wanted to stay. He fired the first shot, and I fired the second one," Jimmy bragged.

"We're proud of you, young man," Wilma said.

After dinner, as if to reward Jimmy, Wilma served fresh baked apple pie, telling him, "You are welcome to stay with us as long as you want to."

"Thanks, but I have to get to a telegraph office somewhere and tell my boss where I am," Jimmy answered.

Walter volunteered, "Well, if you go to mass with us tomorrow, I will introduce you to the manager of the Western Union office in town. Are you a Catholic?"

"No sir, I'm not really much of anything. I buried my mom and dad from a Baptist church, but that's about the only time I went to church," Jimmy answered.

"That's OK. Just go with us anyway. It won't kill you, and I'll introduce you to Charlie Brown, and maybe he can send a wire for you. The Yanks took over his telegraph, but maybe he can figure out a way to sneak a wire off for you," Walter said.

Jimmy enjoyed the night's sleep in the feather bed. He slept better than he had since he'd left Austin. The next morning he put on the best clothes he owned. They were wrinkled from being wadded up in a saddlebag. No matter, he wore them to church with the Wheelers.

Holy Family Church was crowded this Christmas morning. Jimmy was surprised to see so many Union soldiers there. Walter whispered to him, "Their regiment is from Boston, and I hear they have a lot of Catholics there."

Jimmy liked the songs being sung. He assumed they were the same songs they sung in the Baptist church, but they were in Latin. The young-looking priest, Father Jack McGuire, preached a sermon stressing peace and harmony and good will to all men, which he said was the true spirit of Christmas. When the mass had ended a lot of the parishioners gathered in the foyer and talked. The soldiers all left knowing they were unwelcome guests.

Walter looked up Charlie Brown, took him to a quiet spot, and introduced him to Jimmy saying, "Charlie, this young man is a newspaper reporter from Austin and needs to send a wire to his paper. Can you arrange that?"

Charlie shook Jimmy's hand, "I don't know about that. The Yanks guard that key, and even I have to ask permission to use it," he said.

"Jimmy just came here from Corpus Christi, and he actually fought against the Yanks there," Walter quietly told Charlie.

Charlie shook Jimmy's hand again saying, "Somehow we'll find a way. I'm very proud to know one of our combatants."

Jimmy then announced, "If you are willing, I would like to buy us all lunch somewhere. My paper will pay for it."

They agreed, and Charlie knew of a small cafe that was open, so they enjoyed a nice Christmas lunch of roast beef, with mashed potatoes, peas and carrots, black-eyed peas, and iced tea.

During lunch Charlie quietly told Jimmy, "If you can stick around here for a few more days, I hear you will have a good story for your paper. Can you stay?"

"Yes sir. I just will," Jimmy answered.

Wilma interrupted, "Good, we will get to have company for a few more days. It is good to have a young person in the house again."

Walter explained to Jimmy, "What she means is, we have two sons who are off up north with the Army, and we miss them."

"I can understand that. My brother is doing the same thing," Jimmy offered.

Charlie accompanied them back to the WWW Ranch for coffee or bourbon, whichever anyone preferred.

Jimmy and Wilma drank coffee, but Walter and Charlie both preferred bourbon.

After a couple of drinks, Charlie Brown expounded more about his comment on a story developing. He said, "Those damned Yankees have blockaded Galveston ever since the war began. The only things we get from the outside must come by land or from a few smugglers who run the blockade. The Confederates never tried to liberate us. But now, a new Commander, General John Magruder, has taken command and vowed to run the Northerners out of Galveston. My guess is he will do it this week, before year's end."

"Thank you, sir. I'll stick around if the paper will let me. That's why I need to send that wire," Jimmy told him.

"OK, you write it out, and I'll swing by and pick you up after Christmas, and we'll go to town and see if we can get that done," Charlie said.

That evening Jimmy sat talking to Wilma and Walter. Trying to make conversation Jimmy asked Walter, "How many acres do you have?"

Walter answered, "Son, you don't ever ask a man that question. It's like asking him how much money he has in the bank."

"I'm sorry, sir, I didn't know," Jimmy said.

"I know you didn't, and that's OK. I don't mind telling you. We've got 500 acres, all good flat land and rich soil. We produce enough hay to feed our cattle all winter," Walter explained to him.

The next day after Christmas and after breakfast, Walter took Jimmy to a hill overlooking Galveston Bay. Producing a spyglass, he pointed out all of the Federal boats staging the blockade. He showed him the largest vessel and told him, "That is the *Westfield*. It is the flagship." Walter was also able to name some of the smaller ships in the Union fleet.

Walter told him, "I spend a lot of my spare time here watching their ships strut around. I keep hoping some of our ships would come and blow them out of the water."

The following day, as he had promised, Charlie Brown showed up and drove Jimmy into town to try and send a wire. A sergeant was in charge of the telegraph office.

Charlie lied to him saying, "This young man needs to send an emergency wire to his daddy to let him know where he is."

"OK, Mr. Brown. I'm authorized to send emergency wires, but I'll have to send it," the sergeant told him.

Jimmy handed him the message he had written in code.

To Ed Harris—Austin American Statesman
Dear Daddy,
    I am in Galveston staying at the WWW Ranch with Uncle Walter and Aunt Wilma. Would like to stay until the blessed event happens. Please wire back if OK.

Your son,
Jimmy

The sergeant read the wire and asked, "Does your daddy work at the newspaper?"

"Yes, sir. He is a typesetter," Jimmy lied.

The sergeant sent the message and within a few minutes an answer came.

Dear Jimmy,
    Glad you're OK. I was worried. Stay as long as you need to but let me know when blessed event happens. Buy a dinner for your Aunt and Uncle, and I'll pay for it. Be careful.

--Dad

As they rode back to the WWW Ranch, Charlie told Jimmy, "That was pretty good thinking, putting that in code. I'm just glad your boss picked up on it."

"Me too, but I knew he would," Jimmy answered.

Chapter 11

WAR IN GALVESTON

The rest of the week, Jimmy helped out with chores around the ranch. One morning after breakfast, Jimmy rode with Walter. They traveled the perimeter of the ranch, checking to make sure all of the fences were intact. It was almost dark by the time they got back to the house, tired and hungry. They had missed lunch. Wilma was not sure when they returned, so she had not made dinner for them. They settled for ham and cheese sandwiches, buttermilk, and left over apple pie. They were both so tired they went to bed early.

It was still dark, early in the morning, when Walter roused Jimmy saying, "Jimmy, get up. It has started. I have heard cannon fire for the past 15 minutes."

Jimmy slipped into his clothes and joined Walter in the ride to the hill.

Charlie Brown and several others were already there. When dawn arrived, they could see a huge naval battle going on in the harbor. Three Confederate gunboats were attacking the Federal fleet guarding the harbor. It was hard to determine exactly what was happening, but Walter helped identify the ships for Jimmy, who was busy taking notes as fast as he could write. They were able to clearly see one Confederate ship landing a large contingent of infantry on the island. Walter pointed out that one ship had run aground and was soon abandoned and destroyed in a huge explosion. Walter identified it as the *Westfield*, the flagship of the Union flotilla.

They followed the progress of the Confederate troops as they took control of the island. They then crossed the railroad bridge and landed troops in the city.

One of the ladies among those watching from the hill went home and returned an hour later with a large pot of coffee, cups, and a tray of biscuits. She was the hero of the day for the onlookers on the hill.

By three o'clock in the afternoon, the Confederate troops had taken the town and ran up the Confederate flag. The naval battle continued for the rest of the day.

Walter commented, "I wonder if General Magruder planned his attack for New Year's Day, thinking the Irish troops would still be hung over from New Year's Eve."

Thinking it was safe to go into town now with the land battle ended, Jimmy, Walter, and Charlie rode together into the city.

Walter went with Charlie to check on his telegraph office while Jimmy milled about, identifying himself as a reporter, and asking questions of the soldiers and townspeople.

By 5:00 p.m. the naval battle had subsided, and Jimmy entered the telegraph office and asked Charlie Brown to send the following wire to his paper.

> To telegraph operator—Austin American Statesman—Urgent—Urgent—Contact Ed Harris—Have him read this wire and respond to me in Galveston.
> New Year's Day, 1863.
>
> Before dawn today, five Confederate Naval vessels under cover of darkness entered Galveston Harbor. At dawn they engaged the Union fleet there, landed troops, who took control of Galveston Island. They then proceeded to the mainland, defeated the Union troops stationed there, and took control of the city. The entire Union garrison was killed or captured.
>
> The naval engagement also was a victory for the Confederacy. Three Union ships were captured by boarding. Two other Union ships sunk. The Westfield, the Union fleet flagship, ran aground and was blown up to avoid capture.
>
> It was a glorious day for the Confederacy and

the citizens of Galveston who were occupied for four months.

Signed,
Jimmy Dickens, Reporter

Charlie Brown was all smiles as he sent the telegram, then he put his feet on his desk, leaned back in his chair, and announced, "It feels good to have my own office back."

He then reached into a bottom drawer of his desk pulled out a bottle of bourbon and poured a drink for all of them. They toasted the Confederate Army, Navy, and Robert E. Lee. Within an hour Jimmy received an answer to his wire.

> To Jimmy Dickens—Galveston, CSA
>
> Excellent reporting. A real scoop. I'm putting out an extra tonight. Will have a bonus for you. Now come home for a while. Colleen has been here asking about you. Great report.
>
> —Ed Harris

Jimmy invited them all to have dinner with him, as Ed Harris had instructed. Walter went to his ranch to bring Wilma into town, and then the four of them left to have dinner at the Surf and Turf steak house on Galveston Island. At dinner Jimmy showed Harris' wire to all of them and planned to leave for Austin the next morning. He thanked each and every one of them for their hospitality. They celebrated over dinner, as did the entire town of Galveston. By the time they finished dinner, the streets had been cleared of dead bodies, but the glow of ships burning still lighted the harbor. After dinner everyone was tired and in bed early.

Wilma was up making breakfast when Jimmy entered the kitchen in the morning. He had packed his clothes in his saddlebags.

When they finished breakfast he told them good-bye, shook hands with Walter, and got a motherly hug from Wilma, who handed him a lunch she had packed for him.

It was a long, boring ride to Austin, but Jimmy arrived at the paper about 3:00 p.m. the second day. He got a lot of congratulatory handshakes from fellow workers before he got to Ed Harris' office. More congratulations came, and Harris handed him a copy of the extra paper and a check for $100.00. Harris told him to take the coming weekend off and report to work the following Monday.

Chapter 12

BACK IN AUSTIN

This was welcome news for Jimmy. He was tired. He stopped by the bank, cashed his check, and found Colleen waiting for him at the boarding house. She explained, "My mother sent me here to stay with my aunt who lives here. She is ill, and I will stay here until she recovers."

"Well, I'm sorry she is ill, but I'm glad you are here. I have missed you," Jimmy said.

"I have saved both papers with your stories in them. I am so proud of you," Colleen told him.

"Thank you. I am so tired; I need to take a nap. Can you come by tomorrow?" Jimmy told her.

"Sure, I can, but can you just touch me before I go?" she asked.

"Sure, I can," he replied.

"Can I touch you too?" she asked.

"Of course! I really need that too," he replied.

It didn't take long before the two of them were enjoying the touch of each other. Jimmy was the first to enjoy the wonderful climax and issued a loud groan. Colleen soon followed with a quiet scream. Then they held each other and kissed. Before long Colleen told him, "I'm leaving now. You get a good nap, and I'll be over tomorrow," and she left.

Jimmy was so tired he just took off his boots, covered up with the comforter, and slept until the next morning.

The rest of the weekend, Jimmy and Colleen saw very little of each other, with Colleen caring for her sick Aunt.

Jimmy went to the paper early on Monday morning. He was told to report to Ed Harris' office, which he did.

Harris told him, "I sold your story about Galveston to newspapers in Dallas, Houston, San Antonio, El Paso, and Amarillo. It will carry your byline in all of those papers. But what I wanted to tell you is that if you get any job offers from any of them, please give me a chance to match their offer before you take the job."

Jimmy was caught completely off guard, but he replied, "Of course I will, but I am very happy right here."

Jimmy did get offers from Dallas and Houston with a lot more money than he was currently making. He turned them down, and Harris did match the best offer. Jimmy was glad because now he could start looking for a better place to live.

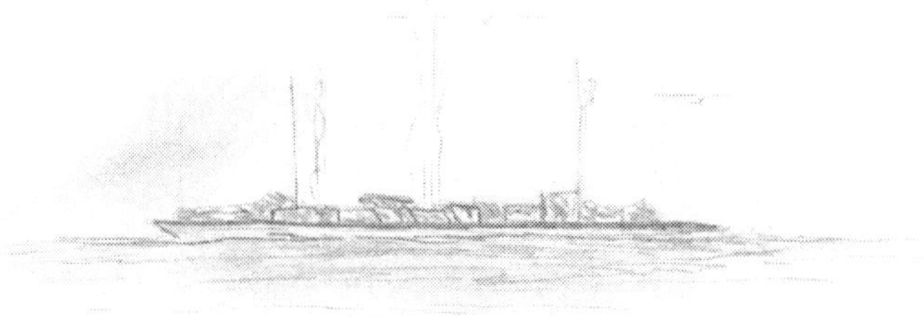

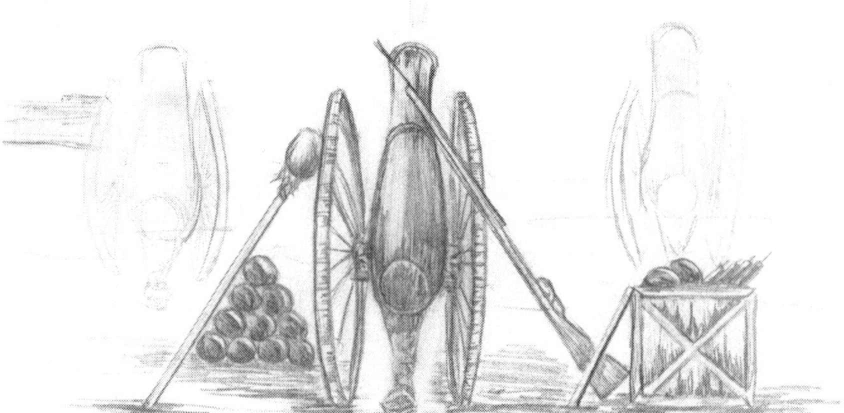

Chapter 13

THE BATTLE OF SABINE PASS

Jimmy spent several months covering local stories, but soon grew tired of the lack of action. He asked Harris for another war assignment, and he was sent to Sabine Pass. He arrived there in July of 1863.

The Texas cotton growers were sending their crops overland to Monterrey, Mexico, where they were shipped to Europe to exchange for war supplies. The Union was committed to closing down this trade route.

In addition to the blockade of Galveston Harbor, the Union also made two attempts to capture Sabine Pass.

Jimmy camped with the mostly Irish "Davis guards," an artillery regiment under the command of Lt. Richard Dowling.

Lt. Dowling was not much older than Jimmy. He allowed Jimmy free run of the camp. Lt. Dowling was red-haired, of stocky build, and a hard-drinking, no-nonsense commander.

To ease the boredom in the camp, Lt. Dowling oversaw cannon target practice. Under all weather conditions, by sunlight or moonlight, the cannoneers practiced shooting at barrels in the mouth of the river.

Lt. Dowling was right there as they practiced, congratulating them on hits, and criticizing them for misses.

Jimmy walked the camp every day talking to the soldiers and asking them if they had been at Sharpsburg and if they knew a soldier named Hans Vogel or Billy Dickens. His efforts were rewarded when one day he met a soldier named Billings, who said he knew both men. He said Hans was a nice man, but Billy Dickens was a son-of-a-bitch who loved killing.

Jimmy stopped his questioning of Billings, lest Billings discover Billy was his brother.

In early September of 1863, a dispatch rider brought news from a Confederate spy in New Orleans that a Union flotilla with 27 ships loaded with 4,000 troops was en route to Sabine Pass. Their mission was to land and secure the area around the Sabine River. If they were allowed to do this, Dowling's force of 46 men would be destroyed, and Port Arthur, occupied.

On September 8, the flotilla entered the mouth of the river, and the roar of Dowling's cannons filled the air. The roar of all of the cannons hurt Jimmy's ears, but he put his hands over them to muffle the noise. He was determined to witness the entire battle. For hours the battle raged. The shore-based cannons were getting off eight shots for every one returned by the fleet.

The practice by Dowling's troops paid off as after the first hour, Dowling's men disabled the lead ship completely, knocking out the wheelhouse. The second hour they disabled the second and third ships, setting them afire. The three crippled ships retreated and the others covered their retreat as they limped back to New Orleans.

Dowling's men gave a loud cheer as the flotilla disappeared from view.

They had suffered only the loss of one cannon and the four-man crew when they received a direct hit from the Naval cannons.

While the cannon smoke was still clearing, Jimmy said good-bye to his newly found friends and rode into the city of Port Arthur.

He had read a great deal about Port Arthur, so was surprised to see a city almost devastated by the Federal blockade. What was once the second busiest port in Texas (second only to Galveston) was now a city in trouble. A lot of the shops were closed, houses were deserted, and commerce had been reduced to almost zero. Nowhere in Texas were the Yankees hated more than in this city.

Jimmy made his way to the telegraph office and struck up a conversation with the operator, Ned Sparks.

Sparks asked him, "Are you a smuggler?"

"No, just a newspaper reporter, and I need to send a wire to my paper," Jimmy answered.

"Well, I just wondered. About the only wires I send anymore are from the smugglers communicating in their own codes when shipments of cotton are on their way to Matamoros, Mexico, to be sent to Europe," Sparks told him.

Jimmy then wrote out his message:

> To Ed Harris—Austin American Statesman
> Just observed the battle of Sabine Pass. Alerted by a message from a Confederate spy in New Orleans. The cannoneers of Lt. Dowling and his first Texas artillery unit engaged a flotilla of Union ships entering the Sabine River. Though only 46 in number and firing only 20 cannons, their superior marksmanship heavily damaged three warships and forced the remaining flotilla to withdraw and return to New Orleans. Lt. Dowling's men suffered only minimum casualties with one cannon and its crew destroyed. This heroic action by the Confederate troops success fully aborted the landing of the 4,000 federal troops aboard the ships and prevented the occupation of this entire area. Lt. Dowling and his men are truly heroes. I'm now awaiting next assignment.
> Signed,
> Jimmy Dickens—Reporter

Jimmy noticed Sparks smiling as he sent the wire. Then he said, "I'd like to buy that Lt. Dowling a drink."

"I'm sure he would accept it. He probably needs one about now," Jimmy said.

Following Sparks' directions, he rode to a hotel called Arthur House, tied his horse out front, and checked in at the desk. The staff was so glad to have a guest in the almost deserted hotel that they sent a man to take his horse to the livery and have him tended to.

Jimmy went to his room and lay down on the too-hard bed and rested. He was exhausted from the excitement of the day. He was almost asleep when he heard a loud rapping on the door. It was Sparks with a telegram for him from Harris. It read:

> Great reporting again, I'm selling your story again. You stay in Port Arthur until I find you another assignment.
> --Harris

He told Sparks, "I just can't wait around here doing nothing. Is there any way you can put me in touch with someone who could arrange for me to get on a smuggler's ship running the blockade and going to Mexico?"

Sparks answered, "I don't know about that. That is mighty dangerous, but if you are serious, I might know someone. Come by the office tomorrow afternoon, and we'll talk about it."

Chapter 14

JIMMY AND THE SMUGGLERS

The next day, with great anticipation, Jimmy showed up at the telegraph office. Sparks greeted him and introduced him to a man who was introduced as Captain Benny Hooks. Captain Hooks was a tall, thin man with a large nose between his coal black eyes. He was completely bald, and he had a red bandana wrapped around his head and tied in the back.

Jimmy thought to himself, *This man looks more like a pirate than a smuggler.*

Hooks asked Jimmy, "You look kind of young. Are you sure you are a reporter?"

Jimmy showed him his press credentials.

"Do you carry a gun?" Hooks asked.

"Yes. Here it is." Jimmy showed his Colt.

"Know how to use it?" was Hooks next question.

"Sure, I do. I used it at the battle at Corpus Christi," Jimmy answered.

"What was a reporter doing actually firing at the enemy?" Hooks asked.

Jimmy answered, "The Colonel in charge told me if I wanted to witness the battle I had to fire at the enemy."

"OK. Now I know who you are. You are the reporter who wrote the article about the battle of Corpus that I read in the *Houston Chronicle*," Hooks responded.

"I am indeed. I wrote the article for my paper, the *Austin American Statesman*, and they sold it to other Texas papers," Jimmy said.

"OK then you're in. Be at the dock tomorrow night. It will be a moonless night, and we will sail at dark. The ship is the *Bluebonnet Belle*, so you can find it. Be there early, and I'll show you around the ship and you can meet the crew. And don't tell anyone where you are going," Hooks instructed him.

"I'll have to notify my boss at the paper," Jimmy told him.

"OK, but do it in code. We don't want to get blown out of the water before we even get into the gulf. And one more thing, if you are going to write about the trip, don't use anyone's real name. We don't need the publicity," Hooks warned him.

After Hooks left, Jimmy wrote a wire to the paper.

> To Ed Harris:
> Austin American Statesman will be out of touch for several weeks. Working on unusual story. In a few weeks I will be saying *"Buenos dias."* Will wire on return.
> --Jimmy Dickens

Then Jimmy told Sparks, "That Captain Hooks is some character. I felt like he thought I was a spy or something."

Sparks responded, "Captain Hooks is a very careful man. He has to be. In his occupation, one moment of carelessness could mean the loss of his life, the men in his crew, and the loss of his ship."

The next day Jimmy packed his clothes, checked out of the hotel, and rode to the telegraph office. Sparks had volunteered to look after his horse and take him to the dock that evening.

Sparks dropped off Jimmy at the docks, wished him good luck, and said he would see him in a few weeks. Captain Hooks saw Jimmy coming, met him, and gave him a tour of the ship. Jimmy was fascinated because he had never been on a ship before.

The *Bluebonnet Belle* was a steam-powered, 51 foot-long frigate. Below decks, Hooks showed Jimmy 200 bales of cotton in the hold. He saw the crew's quarters, a series of hammocks in which the crew slept in shifts.

In the engine room, Hooks showed him the huge boiler that produced the steam. He explained that the boiler had been converted to wood from coal. Wood burned cleaner and left less of a smoke trail than coal. Hooks also proudly showed Jimmy the series of gears that powered the propeller. He also explained if they were being chased, they could change the gears and kick in a second propeller, which would increase their speed by 50%. Jimmy was amazed. Up on deck, Jimmy was shown the wheelhouse, a smoke stack that had been shortened to lower the silhouette of the ship. Two four-pounder naval cannons were mounted on the fore deck and concealed with a tarp.

The crew consisted of two stokers, two deck hands who doubled as cannoners, the captain, first mate, and ten sharpshooting riflemen, who were all armed with Henry repeating rifles. As the ship slipped out of the river into the gulf, they traveled south for half an hour. They had no lights showing and saw no lights from blockade ships, so they turned into the gulf. They stayed well away from the Texas shore, being careful to avoid Port Lavaca and Brownsville, both in Union hands.

After a week on the water they again were in Mexican waters and turned west to go to the Port of Matamoras. They were aware they would be watched by lookouts from occupied Brownsville, so they ran up the British Union Jack flag and covered the name on the stern. The cotton was all in a warehouse, and the crew began sleeping and resting until nightfall. Then they began loading the return cargo of scotch whiskey, tea, muskets, and gunpowder.

It was a good thing the crew was well disciplined and loyal, because they were all tempted by *putas* visiting the dock and offering free tequila and other favors to the seamen. To a man, they turned down the offers and remained on the job.

After the return cargo was loaded, the men again slept and rested during the day until nightfall when they would begin the riskiest part of the voyage back to Port Arthur.

At first Jimmy had a hard time sleeping in the hammock, but the second night he slept well. He didn't know whether he was used to the hammock or if he was so tired he could have slept anywhere.

That afternoon things were quiet and Jimmy had a chance to talk to Captain Hooks.

"Captain, let me ask you about your crew. Do they all work for you?"

Hooks replied, "I'll tell you, but as far as the paper is concerned, the crew are all just volunteers."

"Fine with me," Jimmy replied.

"OK then. Only the stokers work for me. The cannoneers are with the Confederate Navy and the sharpshooters are all a detachment of the Confederate Army. They are all here to guard the shipment of muskets and powder and to transport the munitions to their army unit," Hooks told him.

"What about the rest of the shipment?" Jimmy asked.

"Well, I have a contract with a Houston businessman to deliver the liquor and tea to him. I'm afraid after that the whiskey probably ends up in the hands of less than honest people. I have heard a syndicate controls all of the illegal whiskey and charges a lot for it on the black market. I think you might call them profiteers. I heard the syndicate is controlled by a man named Kennedy, but if I were you, I don't think I would report on that. They are not above killing anyone who stands in their way. But you didn't hear that from me, understand?" Hooks warned him.

"Thanks. I'll keep it to myself," Jimmy answered him.

"Oh yes, one more question. Do you prefer to be called a smuggler or a blockade runner?"

Hooks laughed as he replied, "There is nothing wrong with being a smuggler. After all, John Hancock, one of this country's founders, was a smuggler. He refused to pay the exorbitant taxes the English levied on imported goods, so he bought a ship and smuggled in whiskey and tea. When they finally caught him in Boston and confiscated his ship and cargo, he became a leading force for independence from England," Hooks related.

Jimmy answered him, "I think I'll just call you a blockade runner. It sounds a little nicer," Jimmy told him.

After their ship left Mexico, they sailed well out into the gulf to avoid the ports of Brownsville and Port Lavaca. For the next three nights they steamed north, proudly flying the stars and bars of the Confederacy.

On the morning of the third day the lookouts reported a Union gunboat closing fast on them from the west. In a calm but decisive voice, Hooks ordered the stokers to increase the fire in the boilers and prepare to engage the second propeller when ordered. He then ordered the cannoneers to stand by their cannons and the marksmen at their posts on deck and prepared for action. His orders were instantly obeyed and the deck became a whirlpool of activity.

Within minutes the Union gunboat got close enough to put a cannon shot across the bow of the *Bluebonnet Belle* as a warning to stop.

Hooks then ordered the cannoneers to fire on the closing vessel, then reload and stand fast.

Then the sharpshooters opened fire with their Henry rifles. The barrage they turned loose had the sailors on the enemy vessel ducking for cover and even abandoning their posts at their cannon. Then Hooks gave the order to engage the second propeller, and the Confederate ship lunged forward.

The cannons then fired again as the rifleman reloaded their rifles. A few enemy sailors once again showed themselves but quickly disappeared again when the Henry rifles opened up on them again.

The added speed enabled the rebel ship to outpace the Union ship, and they soon left their opponent far behind. All of the crew then relaxed, stopped the second propeller, and timed their trip so they would arrive at Port Arthur after dark. As they approached Sabine Pass, they saw one more Union vessel, but it was headed away from them, and they were able to slip past it into their dock at Port Arthur.

Safely tied up at the dock, the crew was able to get a few hours sleep before the morning was upon them.

When the morning came, Jimmy said good-bye to the captain and crew and left for the telegraph office to see Sparks. He took him a bottle of Scotch whiskey, which Hooks had given to him.

Sparks greeted Jimmy with a hearty handshake, and Jimmy handed him the Scotch Hooks sent him. Sparks poured each of them a short drink of it. It was too early to drink, but they were celebrating. Jimmy was celebrating the good story he got, and Sparks was celebrating the safe return of his friend, Captain Benny Hooks. Jimmy then wrote the following telegram for Sparks to send to the paper:

> To Ed Harris—Austin American Statesman N.B.
>
> Do not sell this story to Houston Chronicle. Will explain when I get there. This reporter just spent two weeks with 16 of the bravest men I have ever known. The names of the ship and crew cannot be revealed, because they are blockade-runners.
>
> We departed Port Arthur under cover of darkness and were at sea for a week. We finally reached the safety of Matamoras, Mexico, after successfully avoiding the occupied ports of Port Lavaca and Brownsville.
>
> At Brownsville we unloaded 200 bales of cotton for trans shipment to England to exchange for munitions and supplies.
>
> The well-disciplined and loyal crew ignored the

temptations of the port city and remained aboard to oversee and guard the return cargo of muskets, powder, Scotch whiskey, and tea.

During the return trip we were intercepted by a Union ship, but our vessel was better armed and disciplined, and we fended off their attack and outran them. We also dodged another Union blockade vessel at Sabine Pass and finally docked at Port Arthur.

Signed,
Jimmy Dickens
Please advise instructions

Sparks said to him, "You sure had an exciting trip, didn't you?"

"Sure did. But I wouldn't want to do it again. Captain Hooks and his men are braver than I will ever be," Jimmy told him.

Chapter 15

A LETTER FROM BILLY AND A NOTE FROM COLLEEN

Within an hour there was an answer from Harris.

> Great reporting, again. Congratulations. Come on home. Will not sell story to Chronicle but anxious to know why. You have a letter here from your brother Billy.
>
> --Ed Harris

Jimmy was anxious to read the letter from Billy, so he said good-bye to Sparks and set off on the two-day trip to Austin. He arrived at the paper in the afternoon of the second day, anxious to tell Harris about the profiteering he learned about, and to pick up the letter from Billy. Harris sat spellbound as Jimmy recounted the story of Kennedy and the profiteering syndicate.

Harris told Jimmy, "This could be a very large story, but we're going to have to tread lightly. If these people are making millions off of the war, they will go to great lengths to protect their business."

"Yes, my source told me they would kill to protect themselves," Jimmy replied.

Harris handed Jimmy the letter from Billy, and also a sealed note from Colleen. Jimmy took them to the boarding house before he read them.

He opened the note from Colleen and read:

Dear Jimmy,

    I hope you are well. I have exciting news. My aunt died and left me her house here in Austin. She also left me some money, which I am going to use to take classes at the university. I think I can learn to be a secretary in a year or so. When you get this note please come and see me at the house. You know where it is.

I love you, Colleen

Jimmy didn't even take time to refold the note; he just laid it on the bed and ripped open Billy's letter, which read:

Dear brother Jimmy,

    I am writing with bad news. I have been cashiered out of the Army, and taking a job as a materials guard for the Union Pacific Railroad.

    The trouble I had with the Army was not totally my fault. My job was to bring back deserters, dead or alive. They sent me to bring back a Lieutenant Donovan, who deserted in the face of the enemy. I trailed him and tried to arrest him, but he opened fire and I had to shoot back, killing him. I took his body back to camp, draped over his horse.

    Our commanding officer went berserk. He screamed at me, "You have killed an officer. I'll have you court martialed."

    If found guilty I could have been put before a firing squad, so I took the option of a dishonorable discharge.

    I'm sorry Jimmy. I feel like I have disgraced the family name, so I am changing my name to Waco Bill. I don't have an address yet but will be working out of Council Bluffs, Iowa, guarding supplies going to where they are laying tracks for the new transcontinental railroad.

    Please don't disown me, Jimmy. You are the only family I have, and I love you, my brother.

--Billy

Jimmy had tears in his eyes as he finished the letter. That night Jimmy tried to sleep, but he kept thinking about Billy's problems and tossed and turned all night. When he finally woke up, he realized it was Saturday, so he rolled over and went back to sleep. He slept until nine o'clock, when he talked himself into getting up and going to the diner for breakfast.

Then he headed for Colleen's aunt's house. It was a modest wood-frame ranch house, with two bedrooms, a large country kitchen, and a medium-size parlor. As he knocked on the door, Colleen answered and opened it, saying, "Oh, Jimmy! I have been so worried about you."

"I'm sorry, Colleen, but I was at sea for weeks. I was with some blockade runners going between Port Arthur and Matamoras, Mexico," Jimmy explained.

"Well, I have been anxious to talk to you. You told me you wanted to get out of that boarding house, so how about moving in here with me? If you will buy the groceries when you are in town and promise to touch me at least once a week, you can have your own bedroom and I will cook for you and do your laundry," she said.

"It's a deal," Jimmy told her.

She hugged and kissed him, telling him, "Oh, Jimmy! I love you so much." she said.

"And I love you, too" he replied.

That afternoon, Colleen helped Jimmy move his things from the boarding house. That evening Colleen cooked a fine dinner for the two of them, and Jimmy felt more at home than he had since he sold the farm.

They relaxed together all weekend until it was Monday morning, and Jimmy reported for work at the paper.

Chapter 16

THE INVESTIGATION INTO THE SYNDICATE BEGINS

When he walked in the door of the paper, Ed Harris rushed to meet him, "Hey, Jimmy! Get your ass into my office right away. You have a wire here from a Mr. Sparks in Port Arthur. I think you should read it right away."

Harris handed him the wire, and he read:

> Jimmy,
>   Think you should return here immediately. You may have a good story here. Captain Hooks has been shot but will recover. Arms shipment was hijacked enroute to the armory in San Antonio. Six guards killed and four wounded. Wire me if you can come.
>   --Sparks

Jimmy asked Harris, "What do you think, boss? Should I go?"

"Well, I won't order you to go, but if you want to volunteer to go, I will approve it. It could be dangerous," Harris told him.

"I'd like to go. I think I will take the stage to San Antonio, then the train to Port Arthur. It will be a lot faster, and I can hire a horse in Port Arthur," Jimmy replied.

"Just be careful, and keep me informed as to what you are doing," Harris said.

Jimmy left to draw some expense money, send a return wire to Sparks, and go home to leave a note for Colleen.

By noon of the second day Jimmy was back in Port Arthur talking to Sparks.

"What the hell is going on?" Jimmy asked.

Sparks replied, "Just as I told you in the wire. Captain Hooks is in the hospital under police guard with a bullet in his back, and a wagonload of munitions is missing. Six guards are dead, and the four wounded are in a hospital in Seguin with gunshot wounds and under military guard," Sparks told him.

"Oh, shit—I hope my article wasn't the way the assailants found out about the munitions," Jimmy said.

Sparks responded, "I don't believe it was. Nobody here was even aware of the article."

"Do you think I could go interview Hooks?" Jimmy asked.

"Sure, just wait until I get someone to relieve me in the office, and I'll take you to him," Sparks said.

At the hospital, Sparks knew the two police guards, and he and Jimmy were admitted to Hooks' room. They found him lying on his sore back.

"Hello, Captain Hooks. Sorry to see you all laid up like this," Jimmy told him.

"Howdy, Jimmy. The doctors are going to get this bullet out of me tomorrow, and I'll get back to normal soon," Hooks said.

"What in the hell happened to you?" Jimmy asked.

"Just like I told the cops. I was in my cabin, when I heard someone on deck and went to investigate. I only saw a shadowy figure, but then felt pain in my back. Apparently there was another one, and he tried to kill me," Hooks replied.

"Do you think Yankee spies shot you and hijacked the munitions?"

"Hell no—it wasn't the Yankees. It was that damned Kennedy bunch. That damned first mate of mine. Clark was an informant for the Kennedy syndicate. He knew I was catching on to him, so he tried to kill me to shut me up," Hooks related.

"Did you tell the cops about that?" Jimmy asked.

"Oh, hell no, and don't you tell them either. They would finish me off for sure if I told the cops that," Hooks warned.

"Thanks, Captain. We won't say a word," Jimmy reassured him.

Sparks and Jimmy left. When they were alone Jimmy asked Sparks, "Do you think I might be able to interview the wounded guards if I went to Seguin?"

"You might be able to. Why don't you ride down tomorrow and see Lt. Dowling at Sabine Pass and see if he will write a letter of introduction to the guards at Seguin?" Sparks asked.

When he arrived at Sabine Pass, Lt. Dowling was glad to write the following letter for him:

> To Whom It May Concern:
> This letter will introduce Jimmy Dickens. He is a reporter for the *Austin American Statesman*. He was with me during the battle of Sabine Pass when my cannoneers repelled the Union forces and prevented an invasion of Port Arthur.
> He also actively participated in the battle of Corpus Christi. Please extend him every courtesy.
> Signed,
> --Lt. Dowling
> --Commander Cannoneers

Thanking him, Jimmy rode back to Port Arthur to board the train to Seguin the following morning. Seguin was not a regular stop, but a whistle stop. Upon boarding, Jimmy showed his ticket to the conductor, who said he would make arrangements for the engineer to whistle, then stop and let Jimmy off at the Seguin depot.

He was told the hospital was only a few blocks from the depot, so he walked there.

There were two armed soldiers on duty outside the door of the wounded guard's room. Jimmy presented the letter to the sergeant in charge and was granted entry into the room.

Two of the wounded men were conscious enough to speak with him. Sergeant Sweeney and Private O'Leary were both more than willing to relate their experiences. They recognized Jimmy from the blockade running adventure.

Sergeant Sweeney explained, "After traveling all day without a break, we decided to stop at a diner on the western outskirts of Gonzales to eat. Five of the soldiers went into the diner, while the remaining five of us remained on guard at the wagon. When half an hour had passed and the first five had not returned, Private Mullins went into the diner to check on them. He was met with gunfire as he walked in the diner.

"Aware that our primary mission was the safety of the arms, we left immediately. We had only traveled about a hundred yards when a huge log blocked the trail. As we tried to move it out of the way, all four of us were gunned down, and our assailants fled with the wagon load of muskets and powder.

"Fortunately, a nearby farmer heard the shooting, came to investigate, and hauled us in his wagon to this hospital here in Seguin."

Jimmy asked Sweeney, "Were you in uniform?"

"No, sir. We were still in civilian clothes to avoid attention," he answered.

"What was the name of the diner?" Jimmy asked.

"I'll never forget it. It is called 'Mabel's Home Cooked Meals,'" Sweeney answered.

Thanking both of them and wishing them a speedy recovery, Jimmy left to find a horse he could rent to ride to Gonzales to visit the diner. As he rode there, he double-checked to make sure his pistol in the shoulder holster was loaded. He had no idea of what he would find there, but expected it to be a dangerous place.

Jimmy was surprised to see Mabel's. It was a freshly painted white-frame building. He asked for the owner and spoke with Mabel. He asked her, "Mabel, can you tell me what happened here the other day?"

"Are you with the Army?" she asked.

"No ma'am. I am a reporter with the *Austin American Statesman*," and he showed her his press credentials.

"OK. I'll tell you exactly what I told those Army fellers yesterday, but you have to promise not to use the name of my place in your article. I've already had too much bad publicity."

Jimmy promised, so she continued her story.

"Well these five young men came in, ordered coffee and blue plate specials. The next thing I know they were all holding their stomachs and writhing in pain on the floor. The waiter just smiled as they pleaded for help. The army fellers told me they were poisoned."

"Where is the waiter?" Jimmy asked.

"He took off after he shot the sixth young man who came in to check on his friends," Mabel related.

"Had he worked for you long?" Jimmy asked.

"No, we just hired him a couple of days ago. He didn't have any references, but with the war on, we were shorthanded, and needed someone really bad," Mabel said.

"Can you tell me what he looks like?" Jimmy asked her.

"Sure can. He was tall and skinny, had black beady eyes, and coal black hair. He had a hook nose and big ears. He had a black beard. We all used to laugh at him, behind his back, because we all knew the beard was a fake," she told him.

A dawning of understanding was taking place in Jimmy's mind as he listened to Mabel's description of the poisoner. *That sounds exactly like that first mate, Clark. This was indeed a well-planned and executed robbery.*

Jimmy thanked her, finished taking his notes, and left to find a boarding house for the night. He was hungry but was afraid to eat anything at the diner. Soon he found a nice boarding house. Suppertime had passed, but Mrs. Murphy, who owned the place, was nice enough to fix him a sandwich. She also had her teenage son feed his horse and stable him. After he finished the ham and cheese sandwich, Jimmy went to his room and looked over his notes to prepare his story.

At six the next morning he ate a good breakfast of flapjacks and coffee, then rode back to Seguin to return the horse and wait for the next train to Port Arthur.

During the train ride he wrote the story he intended to wire to the paper upon arrival at the telegraph office.

> My last story told of my adventures accompanying a blockade running ship smuggling munitions from Mexico, past the Union blockade and into Port Arthur. Since then the brave ship's captain was shot in the back while protecting his ship. The munitions were loaded into a wagon and accompanied by ten Confederate soldiers enroute to the armory in San Antonio.
>
> When they stopped to eat at a diner in Gonzales, five of the soldiers were poisoned and five shot as the wagonload of munitions was hijacked.
>
> Some of the local people are blaming Union spies, but reliable sources have indicated that the hijackers and murderers were part of a criminal syndicate who stole the shipment of arms for resale to the highest bidder.
>
> Signed,
> Jimmy Dickens
> —Reporter

Upon arrival in Port Arthur Jimmy showed the story to Sparks.

Sparks read the story, and then said to Jimmy, "Wow. This is dynamite. Are you sure you want to file this story?"

"I'm sure. Maybe this will smoke the snakes out of their holes," Jimmy responded.

Jimmy did not reveal to Sparks that he knew first mate Clark was the poisoner and one of the assassins who shot the soldiers.

After the wire was sent, Sparks poured both of them a glass of Scotch.

Sparks remarked, "I sure hope you know what you're doing. I hope you are ready to run for cover or defend yourself. That story is sure to put a big target on your back when the syndicate reads it."

"I'm aware of that, but this will be the biggest story I've ever written, and I'm prepared to take the risk," Jimmy answered.

Sparks poured each of them another glass of whiskey, and before they finished it, a wire came in for him from Harris.

"Dynamite story. Are you sure of your facts? Do you want me to sell the story to the Houston Chronicle?"

Jimmy wired back:

> Sure of facts. Sell story to Chronicle. Let's force the syndicate to come out of hiding.
>
> --Jimmy Dickens

Within minutes Harris wired back:

> OK. It's your funeral. But either come home or go some place and hide out where no one can find you for two weeks. Please be careful. There are sure to be repercussions.
>
> --Ed Harris

As Sparks read the answer he told Jimmy, "That's good advice. If you want to disappear for a while, I have a hunting cabin 20 miles north of here in the piney woods. You are welcome to use it. Go buy yourself some supplies, and I'll take you there after I get off of work this evening. I think you will be safe there."

"Thanks, I'll take you up on that. After stocking up on food, Jimmy purchased a 12 gauge double-barreled shotgun and a box of double-ought buckshot. As Sparks led him through the trail winding through the tall pine trees, Jimmy thought to himself, *No wonder Sparks thinks I will be safe there.*

Sparks opened the cabin for him, then rode towards home after telling Jimmy, "I'll be back here in a week to check on you. Do be careful."

"Thank you. You are indeed a good friend," Jimmy told him.

That night Jimmy felt more alone than he ever had felt in his life.

The bed consisted of a wooden frame with ropes across it to hold the semi-soft cotton mattress. Regardless, when he finally got to sleep, he slept well. His shotgun was laid alongside his bed and his pistol was under his pillow. His final thought before drifting off to sleep was, *I wish Billy was here to keep me company,* and he fell asleep. The solitude of the cabin was relaxing, but the thought of problems that may come later never allowed him to relax completely. The days passed slowly. In other words Jimmy was bored. Some days he chopped wood for the cook stove, but his revolver was always at his side, and he made sure the shotgun was close at hand.

One day he rummaged through some cabinets and came across a book titled *First Blood*. He wondered how Sparks had gotten a copy so soon, since it had only been printed the year before.

Reading through the book, he discovered it was the story of Fort Sumter in Charleston, South Carolina.

A Union officer, Major Robert Anderson, commanded a regiment of Union soldiers stationed in Charleston in a camp on the mainland, on the coast of Charleston Harbor. A new fort was under construction on an island in the harbor. He intended to move his camp to the island once it had been completed.

As rumors of South Carolina's succession from the Union and the declaration of war against the United States grew stronger, he felt he should move to the island. It would make it a lot safer to put water between his men and any attacking force.

Seeking guidance, he sent daily dispatches to Washington.

His dispatches were either ignored or answered by telling him it was his decision. Anderson felt betrayed and alone and wished he was back home in Cincinnati, Ohio.

Daily he felt the winds of war increasing in intensity and decided to move to the island, called Fort Sumter. So as to draw as little attention as possible, he spent the next three nights moving men and armament to the island. As soon as he was beginning to feel settled on the island, the South considered his move an act of war. The South Carolina legislature voted unanimously to secede and declare war on the Union.

The following day cannon fire began, and Fort Sumter was under siege. As Jimmy read the book he thought, *Once again indecision by a bureaucrat caused war to break out.*

Jimmy had been keeping track of his days of seclusion by cutting notches on the hitching post by the cabin door. When he carved the sixth notch, he planned on leaving for town the next morning.

That evening as he was packing his clothes into his saddlebags, Sparks arrived. He brought with him a copy of the *Houston Chronicle* and a long telegram from Ed Harris. He read the paper first. The headline read, "Houston Criminal Syndicate Dealers in Murder, Hijacking and War Profiteering."

Under that was the story he had written. Jimmy then turned his attention to the telegram from Ed Harris:

> Jimmy, you had a visitor here at the paper. Some giant of a man was asking everyone here about you, where you live and how you could be reached. He called himself "Maxie," but the sports department remembered him as a bare-knuckle prizefighter named Slapsy Maxy Bloom. Beware of him. I'm hiring two Pinkerton guards to meet you and stay with you until you come home or until you finish the story there. Let me know where they can meet you. Be careful.
>
> --Ed Harris

Jimmy asked Sparks to reply to Harris telling him he would meet the Pinkertons at the telegraph office on Wednesday. Sparks also handed Jimmy a copy of the *Houston Chronicle*. The first page carried Jimmy's story under a headline, which read, "Houston Crime Syndicate Responsible for Hijacking Confederate Arms for Resale to Highest Bidder."

Sparks explained, "You are the talk of Port Arthur, and no doubt Houston, too. If I were you, I would go home and let things cool off for a while."

"Thank you, Ned. You are indeed a good friend," Jimmy told him.

Wednesday morning Jimmy met with the Pinkertons in Sparks'

office. He told them he wanted to go to Austin, but first would like to visit Captain Hooks in the hospital.

As Jimmy was making plans, the syndicate was also meeting in Houston to formulate a plan to shut Jimmy's mouth forever. The meeting was in Arthur Kennedy's office and was attended by Kennedy, Slapsy Maxy Bloom, and first mate Clark.

Kennedy was an obese man with cheeks so fat they partially obscured his eyes, giving the appearance of a pig's eyes. His gray hair was disheveled and balding in front. He had very small hands and feet, giving the appearance that his body was outgrowing his extremities. He was dressed in a brown western suit with a loud plaid vest.

He was obviously in charge of the group as he said, "Have either of you figured out how to get rid of that damned reporter fellow?"

Bloom replied, "Hell, boss, we have to find him first. I looked all over Austin and can't find but even where he lives."

Clark interrupted, "You find him, and I'll kill him."

Kennedy told him, "I know you enjoy killing people, but you lay low. He knows what you look like."

"I have sent for someone who will be here in about a week or so. He is a professional killer, and I am paying him $1,000 to solve this little problem for us," Kennedy explained.

"Well, we might have one connection to find him. He is friends with Captain Hooks, and we might find him that way," Clark offered.

"Good idea. Hire someone to stake out Hooks' hospital room and see if he pays a visit to the good captain," Kennedy instructed them.

The following morning, Jimmy, accompanied by the two Pinkertons, visited the hospital to check on Hooks. There were two guards on the door again, and they recognized Jimmy and allowed him entry but asked the Pinkertons to remain in the hall. None of them paid any attention to an effeminate male nurse, dressed in white, milling around the hall. Hooks' eyes brightened when he saw Jimmy enter the room.

"Hey there, Jimmy! I see you are quite a celebrity these days," he said.

"Not really, Captain. Just a reporter trying to do his job," Jimmy answered.

"Well, you keep the heat on those bastards. They don't deserve to breathe the same air that honest people breathe," Hooks said.

"I'll sure try. I haven't even mentioned Kennedy or Clark yet, but I will, and that will really piss them off. Now you get well and go back to running that blockade again," Jimmy told him.

"I intend to do that. But you be very careful. Those men would kill you in a New York minute to shut you up," Hooks cautioned him.

Chapter 17

THE INVESTIGATION TAKES A RESPITE

Jimmy and the Pinkertons left the hospital and went directly to the depot to take the train to Houston, then the stage to Austin.

They failed to notice the male nurse following them. He had traded the white uniform for a black slicker and boarded the train in a different car. Upon arrival in Houston, Jimmy and the Pinkertons went directly to the stagecoach stop. The male nurse made his way to Kennedy's office to report his findings.

"Mr. Kennedy! Mr. Kennedy! I followed that reporter and two bodyguards from the hospital in Port Arthur, and they got off the train here. They are in town," he excitedly explained.

"Just calm down, Louis. If they're in town, we'll find them," Kennedy told him.

But he would not find them that day. They were on the Austin stage headed for home.

The three of them went to the paper, and Harris rushed to meet them.

"I'm glad you're home safe. Where have you been hiding?"

"I was in a hunting cabin, several miles from town, and I'm sure glad to be home now," Jimmy replied.

"Well, you had better check in with Colleen. She has really worried about you. By the way, what are your plans now?" Harris asked.

"I'll sure visit with Colleen. I have one more story to write on the syndicate. This time I intend to name Kennedy and Clark as members of the syndicate," Jimmy answered.

"That'll stir them up, sure enough. But before you write it, let me give you some good news. The paper is giving you a membership in the Press Club. Sort of a bonus, I guess. We also are nominating you for the Texas Golden Quill Award. As you know, it is given annually for the best story of the year, and we think you have a damned good chance of winning it. I'd like to take you to the Press Club for lunch tomorrow and introduce you around," Harris explained.

"Wow, Ed. I don't really know what to say. Thank you very much." Jimmy was almost overwhelmed.

Harris told the Pinkertons they were discharged, and he thanked them for bringing his reporter home safely.

Harris had told Colleen about Jimmy coming home, and she picked him up in her buckboard. Jimmy was not prepared for the reception he received from Colleen. She hugged and kissed him like he had never been hugged and kissed before.

"Oh, Jimmy! I have been so worried about you. Mrs. O'Leary from the boarding house came by my house to tell me some giant of a man had been there asking about you. She told him she never heard of you because she figured he was up to no good."

"I'm sorry, Colleen, but I have been in hiding because some bad men are looking for me. The big guy was at the paper also. But no one told him anything, so we are OK," Jimmy explained.

"Well, now you are going to be hiding out at our house," and she prodded the horse forward.

Arm in arm they entered the house. Colleen insisted he sit, and she opened a bottle of champagne for them.

Jimmy said, "Hey, I could get used to this kind of living."

"Well, you had better get used to it because I'm going to spoil you for the rest of your life," she promised. After they drank the better part of the champagne, they began touching each other, but for the first time they were both naked. Colleen touched and kissed parts of him he did not know existed. He did the same to her.

When the touching was over, they both fell asleep still holding each other's naked bodies, and completely relaxed.

The next morning they woke up early, and Colleen busied herself fixing breakfast. Jimmy had to go to work, and Coleen had to attend classes at the University of Texas.

Colleen dropped him off at the paper, then rode on to school

Jimmy was seated at his desk in the open room, but found it difficult to work because of the congratulations heaped on him by his fellow workers.

When lunchtime arrived, Harris retrieved Jimmy and they set out for the Press Club. Jimmy thought the club was the nicest place he had ever been. All of the walls were glass, and it was on the top floor of the Austin National Bank. Jimmy enjoyed the best lunch he had ever eaten. The steak, baked potato, black-eyed peas, and coleslaw were prepared to perfection. This was a far cry from the food he had been preparing for himself at the hunting cabin. He knew he wanted to belong to this club, and looked forward to bringing Colleen there. On the way back to the paper, he thanked Harris for the lunch and told him he hoped he would be voted in as a member.

When they returned to the paper, Jimmy found a telegram waiting for him on his desk. With Harris watching, Jimmy ripped open the envelope and read:

> Dear Mr. Dickens,
> I feel you and your paper have misrepresented me and my associates in your newspaper articles. To prevent a future lawsuit by my firm, I recommend a meeting to try and straighten out any misunderstandings. Please advise if you can come to my office. If you would feel more comfortable elsewhere, suggest a neutral place for the meeting and when you would like to meet.
> Signed,
> Arthur Kennedy

"What do you think, boss?" Jimmy asked.

"I think it's a damned trap," Harris said.

"Surely if he wants to kill me, he wouldn't do it in his own office," Jimmy responded.

"Sure he would. He probably has enough brass to think he can get away with it," Harris answered.

"Maybe I'll suggest a neutral spot. What do you think of the bar in the Menger Hotel?

In San Antonio?" Jimmy asked.

"Well, I think that would be better than his office. But I'm not going to order you to do this, and I won't stop you either," Harris told him.

"Don't worry, boss. I'll take the Pinkertons with me," Jimmy replied. Jimmy then wrote a return wire:

> To Arthur Kennedy, Houston
> From Jimmy Dickens—Reporter, Austin American Statesman
> Will agree to a meeting next Monday at 11 a.m. in the bar at Menger Hotel in San Antonio. Advise if OK.
> --Jimmy Dickens

Within an hour he had an answer agreeing:

> Will meet you in the bar of the Menger Hotel in San Antonio at 11 a.m. next Monday.
> --Arthur Kennedy

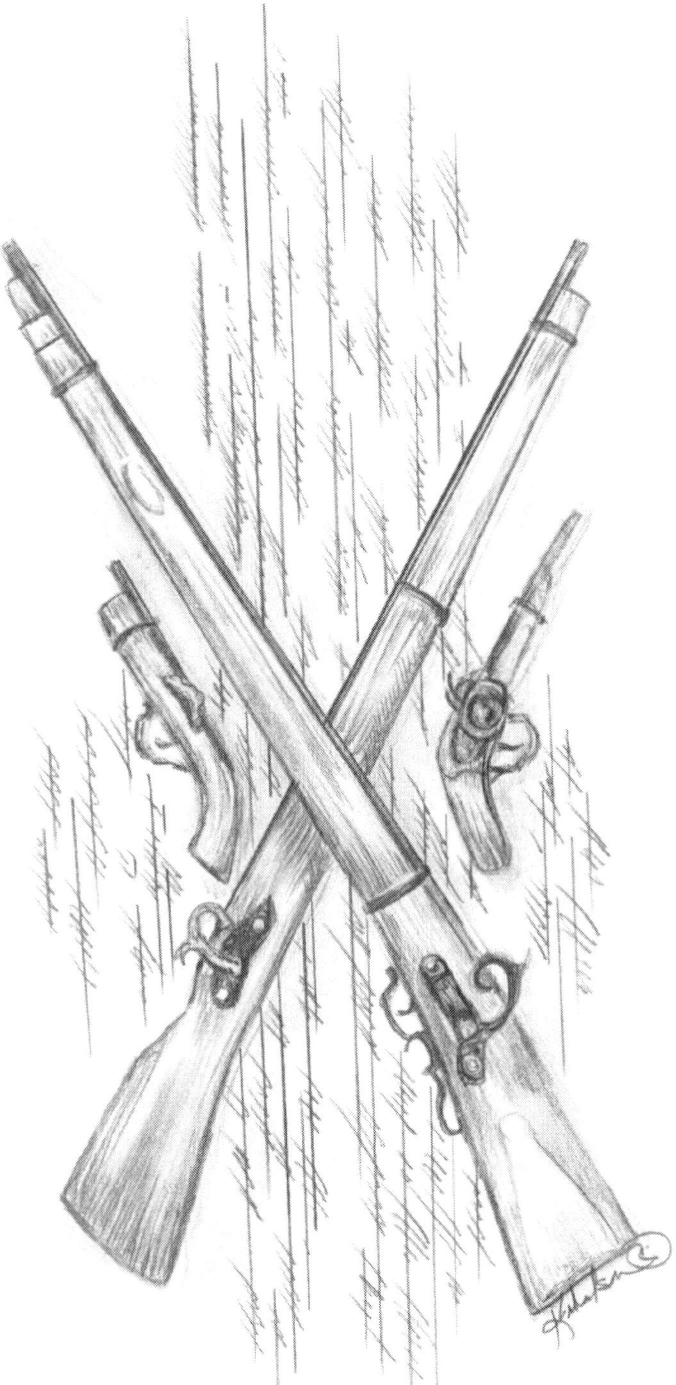

Chapter 18

THE MEETING

Jimmy and the two Pinkertons arrived at the Menger on Sunday. They went into the bar, drank a beer, and checked out the surroundings. They saw in one corner an oblong table where the three of them could sit with their backs to the wall. None of them trusted Kennedy and his cohorts, so they were taking precautions. Jimmy took a room by himself in the hotel, and the Pinkertons shared an adjoining room. The paper was footing the bill, so they did not have to economize.

The next morning they had an early breakfast in the hotel coffee shop. They wanted to be early for the meeting, so after breakfast they were in the bar as soon as it opened. The bartender was very obliging and served them coffee. The only other customer in the bar was a man at the opposite end of the bar starting his day with shots of bourbon. Jimmy noticed very little of the man except he had a full black beard and long black hair protruding from his Stetson.

After several more cups of coffee, a group of three men came in and took a round table next to theirs. Jimmy recognized Clark as one of the three. He also assumed the giant of a man to be Slapsy Maxy. He then assumed the fat man to be Kennedy.

Kennedy spoke first, "And which of you is the reporter Dickens?"

"I am. And who might you be?" Jimmy asked.

"I am Arthur Kennedy, and these are my associates, Mr. Bloom and Mr. Clark," Kennedy said.

Jimmy responded, "Oh, yes. I remember Mr. Clark from a sea trip we were on together."

"Now I want to register a complaint against you and your paper for the lies you printed against me. I have to tell you I will sue if you persist in writing them," Kennedy threatened.

"Sir, I have never mentioned you or Clark by name, but I intend to in an upcoming article," Jimmy told him.

Out of the corner of his eye, Jimmy saw the bearded man at the bar paying close attention and shift position to face the men at the two tables.

"You rotten, little pipsqueak, there won't be an upcoming story," Kennedy said, and reached for a gun under his coat.

Jimmy heard the bearded man yell, "Duck, Jimmy!" and duck he did. After that it was hard to calculate what had happened.

Seven men trading shots at very close range was noisy and deadly. Jimmy did see the bearded man firing, but he was shouting at Kennedy and his men. When the shooting stopped, Jimmy had a wound in his left shoulder, one of the Pinkertons was wounded in the arm, and Kennedy was dead with three bullet holes in his chest. Bloom also died of a head wound. Clark was wounded but would live. The bearded man was also wounded badly and crying out for Jimmy to come to him. When he drew closer he recognized the man as his brother, Billy. Jimmy held him in his arms saying, "Billy, Billy, are you OK?"

"No, Jimmy. I'm dying, but I'm dying happy because I was able to save you."

"Billy—Billy, please don't die! I want us to be together again," Jimmy sobbed.

"Just don't shed tears for me. I'm going to be with Ma and Pa," were Billy's dying words. He gave one gasp and went limp in Jimmy's arms.

Jimmy took off his coat and covered his brother's face, then went to talk to Clark, who was still conscious.

Jimmy told him, "Clark, you stupid bastard. You tried to hire my brother to kill me."

"We didn't know he was your brother. We only knew him as Waco Bill."

By then the bar was surrounded by San Antonio police officers, deputy sheriffs, and Texas Rangers.

Jimmy introduced himself and the two Pinkertons, and explained the bearded man was his long lost brother, Billy. He made no mention of Waco Bill. After he explained who the other three men were, the police chief ordered an officer to fetch a doctor from a nearby hospital.

Police Chief O'Leary was questioning Clark, and Clark was singing like a canary, giving Chief O'Leary names of the syndicate, the location of stolen goods, and even future crimes they planned.

He named Kennedy as the ringleader, but also gave the names of an Army Colonel, an Army sergeant, and a Houston city Alderman who were involved.

Even with the intense pain he was in, Jimmy took notes of all of the names for his next article.

Two doctors arrived. One of them pronounced Kennedy, Bloom, and Billy dead. Jimmy's shoulder wound was not as serious as it appeared. No bones were broken, but some muscles leading to the arm were severed. The arm would be useless for several weeks and would be sore for several more weeks. The wounded Pinkerton had a serious injury to his arm. That would make it unusable for some time, but it would eventually heal completely.

After the doctor bandaged the wound and put his arm in a sling, Jimmy went to talk to Chief O'Leary.

"Chief, I would like to hire an undertaker to prepare my brother and transport his body to the Antioch Baptist Church in New Braunfels. I would like to bury him next to our parents at the cemetery there," Jimmy said, his eyes brimming with tears.

"I know a man who can take care of that for you. I'll send him here to meet you in an hour or so," Chief O'Leary answered.

Then the Chief ordered his men to get a wagon to haul off Bloom and Kennedy. He also sent two men to take Clark to a hospital and keep him under guard 24 hours a day until the doctors released him to be taken to jail.

With things calmed down, Jimmy and the Pinkertons sat at the bar to await the arrival of the undertaker. Jimmy, his hands still trembling, and his eyes still gushing tears, ordered whiskey double shots with beer chasers for all of them.

Jimmy said to the friendly bartender, Bill, "Sorry we messed up your bar."

"Don't worry. That wasn't the first gun battle in there, and I'm sure it won't be the last. But I think that was the loudest we have had. My ears are still ringing," Bill told him.

Shortly, the undertaker, a Mr. O'Dell, arrived, and agreed to Jimmy's arrangements and took Billy's body off in a hearse.

"I'll have him in New Braunfels in three days," O'Dell told Jimmy.

Then Jimmy told the Pinkertons to get them seats on tomorrow's stage to Austin. Then he went to his room to write the story that he would file.

>To Ed Harris—Austin American Statesman:
>
>This reporter along with two brave Pinkerton guards was ambushed by the Houston criminal syndicate we have previously written about.
>
>Arthur Kennedy, Maxy Bloom, and Dick Clark of the syndicate attacked us during a supposed business meeting at the Menger Hotel bar in San Antonio. They had employed a hired killer to assassinate us, but fortunately for us and unfortunately for them, the so-called killer they hired turned out to be my long lost brother, Billy Dickens. When Kennedy started the shooting, Billy began shooting at them instead of us. The result was Kennedy and Bloom dead, Clark wounded, and giving the police details of the syndicate. So far he has named Colonel Joseph Brown, CSA; Sergeant July Jones, CSA; and Houston Alderman Sam Sherman, but I suspect others will be named.
>
>Unfortunately, my brother, Billy, was killed, a Pinkerton guard Sweeney was wounded in the arm, and this reporter received a bullet in the shoulder.
>
>>Signed,
>>Jimmy Smith—Reporter
>
>P.S. to Ed Harris: Please contact Colleen and ask her to contact preacher at Antioch Baptist church in New Braunfels to make funeral arrangements for Billy. His body will arrive there in three days. Also need to get this story in tomorrow morning's paper. This place is swarming with local reporters reporting for tomorrow's edition.

Then Jimmy went to the telegraph office and sent the wire to Harris. He then returned to the Menger bar to talk some more with Bill. Bill got him a sandwich from the coffee shop, and Jimmy ate it with another bourbon, and then went to his room.

Jimmy slept soundly all night, but when he awoke the next morning, his shoulder and arm hurt like hell. The adrenalin from the shoot-out and the whiskey's effects had worn off, but he went with the Pinkertons to the stage stop.

The next afternoon they were in Austin, and Ed Harris met the stage with a two-seated buggy to haul them to the paper.

He congratulated the Pinkertons and told them the paper was paying them a bonus.

He told Jimmy, "Well, young man, you are a pretty popular fellow around the Austin area." Then he held up a copy of the morning paper. The headline was, "Reporter Wounded When Exposing Criminal Profiteers."

Then Jimmy's story followed, under the headline.

Harris also told Jimmy, "I forwarded this information to the Golden Quill committee. If this doesn't make you the winner, I will be greatly disappointed."

"Thank you, Ed. Did you speak with Colleen?"

"Sure did. She is on her way to New Braunfels today. Now you take a couple of weeks off and heal up. Do you want me to drop you off at Colleen's house on the way?" Harris asked.

"Please do and I'll check in with you later on," Jimmy told him.

Jimmy let himself in at Colleen's house. The rough stage ride had his wound bleeding again, and he could hardly wait for Colleen to return so she could change his bandages.

It was almost dark when Colleen arrived. She was careful in hugging him as she said, "Oh, Jimmy! I was so worried about you. I was afraid for you until I read your article in the paper this morning."

He replied, "I'm OK, just shot in the shoulder. But thanks to Billy, I'm still alive."

"Thank God for that. I am so sorry about Billy. I know you two loved each other," Colleen responded.

"Thanks. Did you get to see the preacher?" he asked.

"Of course. I would do anything you wanted me to do. The preacher said he would be honored to have the funeral on Saturday. Do you think you will be able to attend with me?" Colleen asked him.

"Of course I'm going. I hope you will drive me. My left arm will be out of order for a while, and I can't handle a team until it heals," he responded.

"I have already planned on driving you, and we can visit with my family," she said.

The preacher did a terrific job with the funeral. He focused on the heroics of Billy in the service of the Confederacy, and his heroic feat of defending his brother. He ended with the quote, "No greater love has a man than the love of laying down his own life to save the life of a brother."

Jimmy's eyes were welling with tears as the service was concluded.

Jimmy took the preacher aside and talked to him privately.

After Billy was laid to rest alongside their parents, Jimmy and Colleen went to her parents' farm. Her family had been at the service but left before the burial took place.

Her family was glad to see them, and her dad wasted no time in pouring himself and Jimmy a large glass of Irish whiskey. They toasted Billy several times. Then Jimmy took her dad aside and talked privately to him.

Jimmy and Colleen left to get home before dark. On the way Colleen asked him, "What's with all the whispering with the preacher and my dad?"

"Don't be too inquisitive. It was just man talk. You will know soon enough," he answered her.

In the weeks to come, Jimmy's days were spent resting. From time to time he checked in with the paper, but Harris sent him home.

Colleen continued to attend school, but she found time to change Jimmy's bandages every day and do the cooking, cleaning, and laundry.

After three weeks the wound had healed, but his arm was still in a sling. He had trouble using it one hundred percent.

One Saturday afternoon Ed Harris knocked on the door. He came to tell Jimmy he was a finalist in the Golden Quill awards, and he would be expected to attend the awards and banquet at the Press Club on the following Saturday evening.

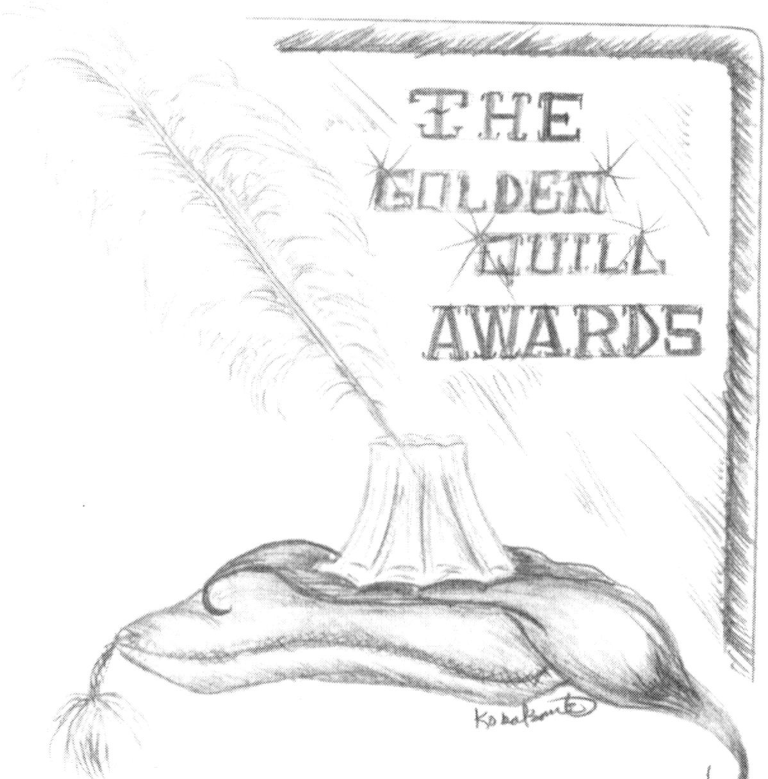
THE
GOLDEN
QUILL
AWARDS

Chapter 19

◆

THE GOLDEN QUILL AWARDS

The Press Club was decorated beautifully. With Jimmy at the table were Colleen, Ed and Mrs. Harris, Howard and Mrs. McGill, the managing editor of the *Austin American Statesman*, and the two Pinkterton detectives who had been at the shoot-out at the Menger. Jimmy had insisted they be invited. Ned Sparks and Captain Hooks had also arrived from Port Arthur.

After coffee and desserts were finished, a Mr. Ben Kincaid took the podium. He announced the three finalists for the award, and asked the finalists to stand when their names were called.

Kincaid was the managing editor and owner of the *Houston Chronicle*, who sponsored the award.

The first name called was Lewis Sinclair, a reporter for the *Dallas Morning Herald*. His story was on the Battle of Gettysburg.

After a round of polite applause, he arose and was recognized, then sat down.

The second nominee was Virginia Lightner. Her story was about the plight of war widows. Again, polite applause as she stood, acknowledged the applause, and then reseated herself.

When Jimmy's name was called, he stood and acknowledged the thunderous applause. Slightly embarrassed, he was quick to wave at everyone, and then sit back down. Colleen hugged and kissed him. Harris whispered to Jimmy, "If the award was for popularity, you would win, hands down."

Then Kincaid opened a sealed envelope and announced the winner: "Jimmy Dickens of the *Austin American Statesman!*" He asked Jimmy to come to the podium. Not expecting to win, Jimmy had not prepared a speech, but he spoke from his heart.

"Thank you all very much. I really should share this award with a lot of brave people who helped me gather information for this story.

"My thanks to Ned Sparks, who guided me to the blockade runners and later hid me when the criminals were looking for me.

"Thanks also to Captain Hooks, who allowed me to accompany him on a run through the blockade and later tipped me off to the criminal conspiracy. To four brave confederate soldiers, who were wounded protecting the munitions. To my boss, Ed Harris, who gave me the latitude to pursue the story. To the two brave Pinkertons, who protected me and helped destroy the criminal cartel. To my late brother, Billy, who was hired to kill me but instead killed the men who wanted me dead. And last but not least, Colleen Sweeny, who cared for me and whom I intend to marry, if she will have me."

Colleen rushed to the podium, kissed Jimmy and said, "Of course I will. I love you."

The applause was thunderous, and Colleen stayed with him as he accepted the Golden Quill Award.

It was a beautiful quill fashioned from gold and set in a crystal base and inkwell.

He was also handed a check for $10,000. He had no idea a cash award was involved. Harris had neglected to tell him about it.

After a lot of congratulatory hugs, handshakes, pats on the back, and well-wishing, Jimmy and Colleen rode home.

Colleen said, "Jimmy, what a stinker you are. What a way to propose, but I love the way you did it. I love you so much."

"And now you know what all of the man talk was about. I asked the preacher if he would marry us, and I asked your daddy for permission to marry you," Jimmy told her.

That night they went straight to the bedroom, undressed each other, and began kissing and touching. This time it would not stop with touching, but at long last with the act of love making, and the union was consummated.

Chapter 20

◆

JIMMY TAKES ON A NEW ASSIGNMENT

It was Sunday afternoon, and Jimmy and Colleen were relaxing at home, reading the newspaper and making plans for the upcoming wedding. The quiet of the afternoon was interrupted by a loud banging on the door. It was Ed Harris. He rushed in shouting, "Sorry to interrupt you two lovebirds, but Jimmy is still a reporter, even if he is a Golden Quill winner." Harris was a good and fair boss, but he was also a hard-boiled newspaperman who was demanding of his employees.

Jimmy rushed forward and shook the outstretched hand extended to him and said, "Yes, sir, boss! What do you need me to do?"

Harris told him, "From the dispatches I have been getting from up north, it looks like the war is almost over, and we are going to lose."

Colleen spoke up, "Oh, what a shame."

"Yes, it is a crying shame, but now we have to face reality. I also got word we might still be sending forces to south Texas to drive the Yankee soldiers out of there. Jimmy, I need you to go down to Palmetto Ranch, east of Brownsville. Then after that assignment is finished, go on to Houston and cover the trial of the syndicate of war profiteers," Harris explained.

"Yes, sir. When do I leave?" Jimmy answered.

"Tomorrow morning. Come by the paper, bright and early tomorrow, and get some expense money and get on your way to Brownsville. Colleen, I am sorry, but your man may be gone for several months. By the way, when do you finish your secretarial studies?"

"In three weeks," she answered.

"Good. When you finish, come by the office and see me. We might have a job for you," Harris told her.

As he left, Harris told Jimmy, "I will be expecting another good story or two out of you, so don't let me down."

"You can count on me, and thanks for the opportunity and for thinking about Colleen," Jimmy answered.

After Harris was gone, Jimmy saw that Colleen was on the verge of tears, so he told her, "Please don't be sad. This is another good opportunity for both of us. Time will fly by, and you can busy yourself with finishing school, starting a new job, and spending your spare time making wedding plans for us. I will be home before you even miss me."

"I doubt that, but I understand that's what being in love with an ace reporter is, and I'll just have to put up with it," she answered.

The next morning, Colleen waited in the buggy as Jimmy went in to the paper to get instructions and expense money, then drove him to the stage station and kissed him as he boarded the stage to San Antonio. Then she drove herself to school. To drive away her sadness, she kept reminding herself how fortunate the two of them were. They were no longer on the farm, they had each other, and had a comfortable life. Indeed, God had been good to them.

Her first class that morning was typing, and she was glad of that. Having to use her fingers as well as her mind helped keep her from thinking about how long it would be until she saw Jimmy again.

By the time the stage arrived in San Antonio, Jimmy was too late to catch the stage to Brownsville, so he checked into the Menger Hotel for the night. As he sat at the bar drinking a beer before supper, his mind traveled back to his last visit there when he got wounded and his brother, Billy, was killed saving his life. *Enough of these crummy memories*, he thought, and then he finished his beer and went to the coffee shop for a sandwich.

He sat in the room carefully recording his expenses of the day into his journal. Then he cleaned and reloaded his Colt and went to bed. At first he had trouble getting to sleep, so he reminded himself he had to be up early to catch the 6:00 a.m. stage to Brownsville. He forced his body to relax, and soon was able to drift off to a restful sleep.

The next morning he woke up at five, washed his face and hands in the basin, dressed hurriedly, ate a biscuit, washed it down with two cups of coffee, and was seated on the stage coach by five-forty five. The only other passenger was a middle-aged lady, who identified herself as Shirley Ranker, a schoolteacher. She was on her way to the T Bar M Ranch to act as a private tutor for the McClain family's two boys, Mike and Craig.

Jimmy told her he was a reporter with the *Austin American Statesman* and was enroute to Brownsville in search of a story. He had learned not to discuss his assignment with strangers.

She surprised him by saying, "Oh, you mean that southern army that is on its way to run the Yankees out of south Texas?"

Showing his surprise by the puzzled look on his face, he asked her, "Yes, but how in the world did you know that?"

"It is not some deep, dark secret. Everyone in south Texas knows it is going to happen," she explained.

Two days later they arrived in McAllen and Jimmy went straight to the telegraph office and sent the following wire to his paper:

> To Ed Harris, Austin American Statesman:
> Everyone here aware of upcoming battle. If I wait for Friday's stage will miss action, so I am renting a horse here and riding to Brownsville. Will wire from there.
> --Jimmy Dickens
> LTC

Within half an hour Jimmy had a return wire from Harris:

> Jimmy Dickens, Reporter—McAllen, Texas
> Not surprised at widespread knowledge of upcoming battle.
> Get there fast and send report of battle including casualties.
> Will give your love to Colleen.
> --Harris

When reading the wire, he thought, *Well, I'll be damned!* Harris had already broken the LTC code that he and Colleen had only made up the night before he left. *It is impossible to put anything over on that old man*, he decided.

Jimmy hastened to rent a horse from the livery and rode towards

Brownsville at a fast pace. On the western outskirts of town, he found a boarding house, and after caring for his horse he took a room for the night. Mrs. McGonigal, the owner, asked him what he did for a living.

When he told her he was a reporter, she advised him breakfast would be served at six, and that he should eat fast and ride east because the battle would begin that next morning.

Word sure spreads fast in south Texas, he thought.

The next morning at the breakfast table a young man introduced himself as Mac McGonigal, the son of the owner. He said, "Hey, mister. Ma says you're going to the battle. Give me fifty cents, and I'll guide you over there and back."

"It's a deal," Jimmy told him, and after breakfast the two of them left for an area called Palmetto Ranch.

During the ride there, Mac said, "I've been coming over here every day for a week and watchin' what's going on. The Yankees are anxious to get off of Brazos Island, but our troops have been watching them and just waiting for them to try it. I hope we wipe them out once and for all so there ain't no Yankees in Texas no more."

Even before they reached the spot where Mac thought the battle would be fought, they heard the distant rumble of cannon fire.

Jimmy asked, "Is that cannon fire I hear?"

"Sure is. It has started," Mac replied.

They spurred their horses, anxious to get closer and find a good vantage spot to witness the battle. From a small knoll they watched as Union forces attacked a Confederate camp, routed them, and proceeded to torch the arms and supplies they left behind. Though the rebels fought bravely, the overwhelming opposition forces had them in full retreat.

By mid-morning, however, Confederate reinforcements arrived and the two sides formed into two skirmish lines, where they would battle until night fell.

Jimmy told Mac to get on home so his mother wouldn't worry, paid him fifty cents, then fashioned a bed from his horse blanket and used his saddle for a pillow. He was soon asleep.

He was awake early, his sleep disturbed by his hunger and the noise of the resumption of the sounds of the battle below him.

He carefully watched the battle and was taking notes when something memorable happened. A detachment of Mexican soldiers crossed the river and attacked a group of Yankee soldiers, then recrossed the river into the safety of Mexico.

Jimmy's attention was distracted from the battle when a lone rider approached. It was Mac with a huge basket of sandwiches and a large pot of coffee.

Mac said, "Momma thought you might be hungry. I ate last night but I know you didn't, so she sent some food for you."

"God bless her, and God bless you for bringing it here for me," Jimmy told him, in between hungrily wolfing down a sandwich and slurping the coffee.

"How is the battle going?" Mac asked.

"It looks like we are winning. One strange thing happened just before you got here. A mounted detachment of Mexican soldiers rode across the Rio Grande and shot at the Union soldiers. Then they rode back across the river," Jimmy related.

"Look down there and you'll see why," Mac said, pointing to a large detachment of black Union soldiers. "Mexicans just don't like black people. I don't know why. I asked Momma, but she didn't know why either."

As the two of them continued to watch, the Confederates sent a force along the side of the Union skirmish line in an attempt to block the line of retreat for the Federal troops. Seeing this, the Union commander ordered a forward skirmish line established, while he led the rest of his command in an orderly retreat to the safety of Brazos Island. After that the Confederates attacked the forward skirmish line and killed, wounded, or captured the remaining soldiers.

"Looks like it's all over," Jimmy commented.

"'Peers so," Mac agreed.

As if to celebrate the Confederate victory, Mac and Jimmy finished off the coffee and sandwiches.

Then Mac volunteered, "Oh I forgot to tell you, but Momma said to tell you the war is over. General Lee surrendered to General Grant weeks ago. It was in the Brownsville Gazette last evening."

"Well, I'll be damned. Then all of this was for naught!" Jimmy blurted out.

"Guess so," Mac answered.

Then Jimmy instructed Mac, "You go on home now and tell your mother I am going to hang around here for a couple of days and talk to the soldiers and get some more stories for the article I have to write. Tell her I will be back at your house in a day or so and settle up with her."

Mac rode off for home and Jimmy rode down to the battlefield. He approached the first soldier he saw, a corporal, who took him to see the commanding officer.

Colonel John Ford asked him, "Who might you be, young feller, and what in the hell do you want here?"

"Sir, I am Jimmy Dickens, a reporter with the *Austin American Statesman* paper, and I watched the battle from that knoll over there." He showed the Colonel his press credentials.

Satisfied, the Colonel offered him a drink of liquor from the jug he had been drinking from, and said to him, "Your horse looks plumb tuckered out."

"Yes, sir. He is. I haven't been able to feed him since yesterday," Jimmy replied, as he took a drink from the jug.

"Well, as an old cavalry officer, I hate to see a horse in that shape. Corporal, take this man's horse. Feed, water, and curry it, then report back here to me," Ford commanded.

"Yes, sir," and the Corporal led the horse away.

Jimmy asked for and was granted permission to camp with the troops and interview them. Then Colonel Ford told him, "Just call me Rip; that's what everyone else does."

Jimmy asked him, "Rip, did you know the war was over before the battle started?"

"Sure I did, and so did that damned Yankee Colonel Ted Barrett, but the son of a bitch attacked anyway. I guess the festering sore of war built up over four years takes a long time to heal," Rip told him.

"What about those Mexican soldiers crossing the river to help you out?" Jimmy inquired.

"I would just as soon you not put that in your paper. We don't need to cause some international incident. We have to live with the Mexicans long after all of those Yankees have gone home," the Colonel warned him.

"Agreed," Jimmy responded, and set about interviewing the Confederate soldiers and the Yankee prisoners.

That night Jimmy ate and slept with the troops and again slept on his horse blanket with his saddle for a pillow. His last thought before sleep engulfed him was, *Tomorrow night I will sleep in a bed.*

Early the next morning he said his good-byes and thanks and left for Brownsville. There he found a quiet table in a saloon and worked on his story as he sipped a beer. Later that afternoon he composed the following lengthy wire to his boss:

> To Ed Harris, Austin American Statesman, Austin, Texas:
>
> After interviewing Confederate combatants and Union prisoners held by the Southern forces, I was able to piece together the following story:
>
> Even aware that Lee had surrendered to Grant on April 9, Union Colonel Ted Barrett led his forces from Brazos Island to the mainland of Texas on May 11. His force was composed of 250 men of the 62nd U.S. colored regiment and 50 men of the 2nd Ohio's cavalry regiment. They first surrounded a rebel outpost at White's ranch but found it abandoned. The troops were exhausted from the long march and were ordered to take shelter in the reeds along the Rio Grande River and sleep.
>
> About 7:00 the next morning someone on the Mexican side of the river saw them and sent word to the Rebels. Second in command to Barrett was Lt. Colonel Branson, and he ordered the command to attack the Confederate camp at Palmetto Ranch. By noon they had overwhelmed the Rebels. Their fortunes were reversed by 3:00 p.m. when a large Confederate force commanded by Colonel John Ford appeared and drove the Union forces back, even after they had been reinforced by 300 men of the 34th Indiana volunteer regiment. The relentless cannon fire of the Rebel forces had forced Barrett to set up a forward skirmish line and lead his men to retreat. Colonel Ford saw this tactic and tried to cut off the retreat, but Barrett successfully withdrew to the safety of Brazos Island. Two Union soldiers were killed, 6 were wounded, 102 captured, and two are listed as missing. It was believed they had escaped into Mexico. Among the Union dead was Private John J. Williams. He would be the last casualty of the Civil War.

Confederate soldiers fared much better with only one dead and five wounded.

Then Colonel Ford ordered the dead to be buried and the prisoners released, then disbanded his unit and told the soldiers to return to their homes.

Even if we lost the war, we won the last battle.
--Jimmy Dickens, Reporter
Reply to me at McGonigal Boarding House, Brownsville.
LTC

After sending the wire, Jimmy rode to the boarding house hoping he would be in time for dinner. He was. It was soon after Jimmy enjoyed a delicious dinner of brisket, green beans, and cornbread, when a rider arrived with a telegram from Harris. It read:

Great job. Yours wasn't first, but by far the most detailed. Now get to Houston ASAP.

Profiteering trial set to begin next Monday. Wire when settled there. Colleen says your love is returned.
--Ed Harris

The next morning after a deep sleep in a comfortable bed, Jimmy ate breakfast, paid Mrs. McGonigal, gave Mac an extra dollar for his help, and rode off for McAllen. There he returned his hired horse and boarded the stage for San Antonio. From there he took the train to Houston.

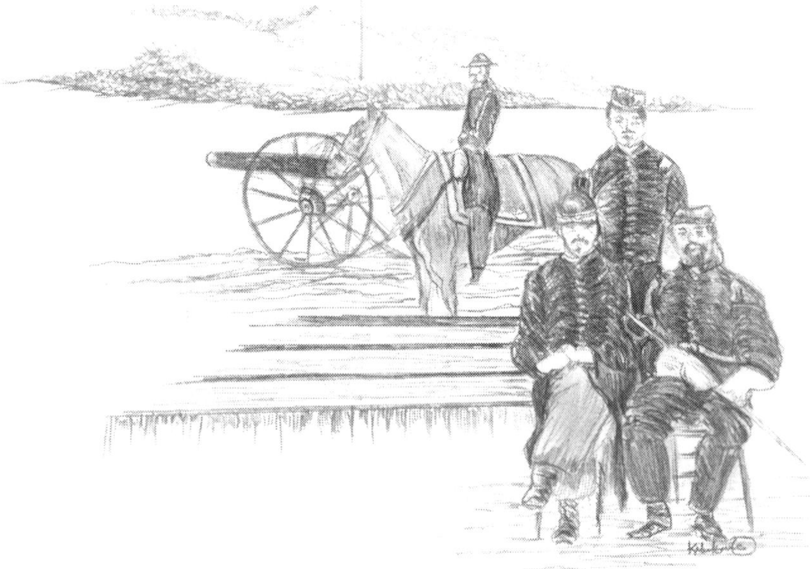

Chapter 21

THE PROFITEERS GO ON TRIAL

Jimmy was tired when he arrived at the train depot in Houston. He tried to sleep on the train, but the noise from a group of school children kept him awake. They were being treated to their first train ride, and enjoying it immensely.

Jimmy hired a buggy and driver and inquired about a hotel close to the Harris County Courthouse. The driver reported there was the Savoy Hotel a block from the courthouse, but they charged $4 a night. Thinking he had earned it, Jimmy asked the driver to take him there.

The Savoy was nice, but he thought the Menger was better. After he checked in, he went to the bar and drank a bourbon before having dinner in the coffee shop, and then he went to his room, undressed, and soon was sound asleep on the soft bed.

He still had two days before the trial began, so the next morning he had breakfast in the coffee shop, then walked to the courthouse. It was not an impressive building, only a two-story brick structure with lots of windows. The windows would be absolutely necessary in the summer to allow air into the building. Otherwise, the building would be unusable in the Houston summer heat.

He went through the massive wooden doors and looked at a courtroom on either side of the anteroom. The room on the left was marked "Courtroom A: Judge Benjamin Serey."

On the right the room was marked "Courtroom B: Judge William Bennett." In an empty office he found a bailiff drinking coffee and asked him, "Which courtroom will the profiteers' trial be in?"

"Courtroom B with Judge Bennett. Are you a lawyer?" the bailiff answered.

"No, I'm a reporter. My name is Jimmy Dickens, with the *Austin American Statesman*," Jimmy answered, extending his hand.

The bailiff took his hand, shook it, and said, "Oh, sure. I have read some of your stuff— nice to meet you. I am Emmett Evans, and I am Judge Bennett's bailiff. Did you hear the latest about the trial?"

"I haven't heard anything," Jimmy answered.

"Well, Judge Bennett has just approved the defense request to allow all three defendants to be tried together. Clark will still have to be tried later on the murder charge," Evans explained.

"Thanks a lot. I appreciate the information," Jimmy answered him.

Then as Jimmy left, Evans said to him, "Let me know if there is anything I can do for you."

"Thank you, sir. See you tomorrow." And Jimmy left.

When he reached the hotel, he wrote this wire to the paper:

> To Ed Harris, Austin American Statesman, Austin, Texas
>
> Arrived in Houston yesterday and checked in at Savoy Hotel. Hope it is OK.
>
> Trial of profiteers begins tomorrow and will be in Courtroom B, with Judge William Bennett presiding. Have learned Judge Bennett has just approved defense request to allow Clark, Colonel Brown, and Sergeant Jones to be tried together, instead of separate trials. Clark will have separate trial later for multiple murder charges.
>
> Will wire again after trial begins.
>
>   Jimmy Dickens, Savoy Hotel
>   Houston, Texas
>   LTC

Jimmy then gave the wire to a bellboy to take to the telegraph office and went into the coffee shop for lunch. Even before he finished his second cup of coffee after lunch, the bellboy returned with an answer from Harris.

Savoy is fine. Paper has an account there. Just show credentials at desk and they will bill paper direct. Good reporting on trial. Colleen graduated last Friday. I represented you in your absence. After seeing her grades, I hired her as my secretary, but my boss overruled me. She is now secretary to Ralph McGill. She says she will write you this week.

The next morning Jimmy had an early breakfast and headed for the courthouse. He was met by Emmett Evans, who told him, "Hi Jimmy. I'll have to keep your Colt for you. No guns in the courtroom except mine, and the judge probably has one under his robe."

"Howdy, Emmett. That's fine. Where do I sit?" Jimmy asked.

"The press section is up front on the right side," Evans explained.

Jimmy had just been seated when he was approached by another occupant of the press section. Jimmy remembered him as the man who had presented the Golden Quill Award to him, Ben Kincaid, managing editor of the *Houston Chronicle*.

"Hello, Jimmy. Do you remember me?" he asked.

"Of course I do, Mr. Kincaid. How are you?"

"I am fine, but I would be better if you would quit that hick town paper you work for and come down here and work for me at *The Chronicle*."

Jimmy was dumbfounded and took a minute to answer. "Thank you, sir, but I am very happy right where I am."

By the time the court was called to order, the press section was almost filled with reporters. When Judge Bennett came in and sat, Jimmy made a point of studying him very carefully. He was a man in his fifties, slightly overweight, had graying black hair, and a carefully trimmed mustache. It was hard to make out the color of his eyes because of the Prince Nez glasses he wore. He had a slight sneer on his face, which Jimmy suspected was a permanent feature.

The prosecutor, Tom Banks, opened the proceedings by reading the charges against the defendants: conspiracy to commit murder, conspiracy to steal government property, and war profiteering.

Tom Banks was a man who was less than six feet tall and of a slight build, but he had a booming bass voice that resonated in every corner of the room when he spoke. One of the jurors, who wore an ear trumpet, removed it when Banks was speaking.

Captain Hooks was the first witness called to testify. He testified that he was under contract to Arthur Kennedy to run the blockade and deliver tea and liquor to the firm owned by him. He testified that he also had a contract with the Confederate Army to bring arms and munitions through the Union blockade. He also stated it was common knowledge on the docks that Kennedy also belonged to a syndicate that was profiteering on goods. So far there had been no objection from either of the two defense attorneys, Haines and Calhoun.

Judge Bennett also noticed the lack of objections and asked, "Don't either of you defense attorneys have any objections to this testimony?"

"No, Your Honor. We have only heard testimony against Mr. Kennedy, not our clients."

Then the prosecution called Mrs. Mabel Jones, owner of the diner where the robbery started. She testified that Clark worked as a waiter at her diner. She testified he had poisoned the first five soldiers who came in to eat and shot the sixth soldier, who came in to check on the other five.

Unlike the treatment Hooks received, her testimony was constantly interrupted by loud objections. Haines objected to her saying the soldiers had been poisoned. He also questioned how she was able to identify Clark as the poisoner. The objections were overruled after Banks produced an affidavit from the doctor who examined the bodies. He reported they definitely were poisoned.

Mabel also overcame the objection to identification by explaining that despite the fake beard he wore, she could identify him by his beady eyes and protruding ears.

The next testimony came from Sergeant Sweeney, one of the guards who were wounded during the ambush that took place further down the road. He testified that when Clark came out of the diner shooting at them, he ordered the wagonload of munitions to drive off, not knowing more danger was ahead in the ambush. There were no objections to his testimony.

With this part of the trial completed, Judge Bennett ordered a break for lunch.

Jimmy invited Evans to join him for lunch, and they walked together to the Savoy.

During lunch Jimmy inquired how Evans got to be a bailiff. He was completely surprised by the answer he received.

"I was a corporal in Grey's Texas Regiment and took a minnie ball in the shoulder at the Battle of Sharpsburg. I ended up in a Yankee hospital, and in the bed next to me was a Colonel Bennett. We became friends and were both sent home in a prisoner exchange. He became a lawyer, and I took a job as deputy sheriff of Harris County. Then when he became a judge, he asked me to be his bailiff, and I jumped at the chance."

"Then you two have been friends for a long time," Jimmy told him.

"Very true. I would do anything for him, and I feel like he would do the same for me."

After lunch they walked back to the courthouse with Jimmy having a better understanding of the relationship between the judge and his bailiff.

Then Jimmy inquired about the Houston City alderman, Sam Sherman, who was named by Clark but was not standing trial.

"Oh, that crooked bastard. Before he could be arrested, he blew his brains out in his outhouse. He was a coward," Emmett told him.

"I would say the outhouse was a fitting place for a piece of shit like him, who betrayed the trust of the honest people who elected him," Jimmy commented.

Evans laughed.

When they arrived at the courthouse, the trial was about to resume.

Next to testify was a Union Army lieutenant. He testified that he led a unit of Union soldiers to take possession of the hijacked munitions hidden in a deserted barn on the outskirts of San Antonio, exactly where Clark said they would be.

The defense team then asked him, "Why were you so anxious to recover the munitions?"

"Well, sir, we knew the Mexican Army had already paid the syndicate for the arms, and we didn't want them to get them in their hands," was the answer.

Haines then interjected, "Then I guess you could say Mr. Clark did a service for the Union Army when he disclosed the location of the munitions."

"I wouldn't say that. He was only trying to save his own neck. He couldn't have known the war was going to be over this soon," the sergeant responded.

That ended the prosecution's case.

The defense then introduced a barrage of character witnesses who testified what good, honest, upstanding citizens all of the defendants were.

Jimmy looked at Judge Bennett and noticed he was so bored that he was almost dozing off. No doubt he had heard this endless parade of mundane, ineffectual nonsense too many times before.

After Judge Bennett grew tired of too many witnesses, he adjourned the trial until 9:00 a.m. the following morning.

Jimmy, in an effort to avoid having to talk with Kincaid again, made a quick exit and walked quickly to the Savoy. After a quick glass of bourbon in the bar he went to his room and prepared a wire and reported the day's proceedings to the paper.

He began the wire by telling of the day's testimonies, especially the damning testimony of Mabel Jones and Captain Hooks. He then editorialized about Judge Bennett's obvious boredom at the testimonies of the defense's pathetic-sounding character witnesses.

Then he added that he also learned the fate of Sam Sherman, the Houston City councilman, which he was named by Clark as a member of the syndicate but had not been present at the trial. He shot himself to death rather than face the embarrassment of a trial. Then in closing Jimmy told of his conversation with Ben Kincaid.

After sending the wire, he adjourned to the bar and ordered another bourbon. Before he had a chance to finish his drink, a bellboy came in and handed him a wire from Harris.

It read, "Splendid job. Glad you uncovered fate of Sam Sherman. Wondered why there had been no mention of him lately. About Kincaid, you have to make up your own mind, but I would advise you that your best future would be right here with this paper. Harris"

As he finished the wire he thought, "Uh oh. I guess I should have mentioned I turned Kincaid down."

Tired from sitting in the courtroom all day and relaxed from the two bourbons, Jimmy went to his room and went to bed.

Early the following morning, he had a leisurely breakfast and walked to the courthouse.

He was relieved Kincaid was not seated in the press section, so he took a seat and watched as Judge Bennett gaveled the court into session.

Most of the morning was taken up with the prosecutor summing up the evidence, and asking the jury to bring in a verdict of guilty. He asked them to impose the maximum penalty of ten years to each of the defendants.

Then the defense attorneys claimed all of the evidence was false, the testimonies of the prosecutor's witnesses were coerced, and the entire case against the defendants was the product of an unscrupulous newspaper reporter trying to make a name for himself.

Hearing this, Evans smiled, looked at Jimmy, and winked.

When court was adjourned for lunch Jimmy asked Evans, "Want to have lunch with an unscrupulous reporter?"

"Only if you promise not to write any lies against me," Evans joked. As they sat down for lunch, Evans' mood changed from jovial to dead serious.

"Jimmy, I have to ask you a favor. The judge believes there is going to be trouble if the defendants are found guilty, as they are sure to be, and so do I," Evans said solemnly.

"Trouble from whom?" Jimmy asked.

"From more syndicate stooges. You know we never did apprehend the robbers who actually attacked the wagon, took it, and hid it. We couldn't ever find them because only Kennedy knew who they were. Now with him deader than a door nail, we have no clue as to their identities and where to look for them."

"But what can I do to help? You have my gun locked up," Jimmy inquired.

"Well, when we get back I'll stick your Colt in my belt, under my coat, and if anything breaks out, I'll toss it to you, and you can watch my back," Evans said.

"I'll do it," Jimmy promised. Then they finished lunch and walked back to the courthouse.

When the trial resumed, the judge ordered the jury to retire and deliberate the fate of the defendants. Evans escorted the jury out and stood guard at the door to guard them and to make sure no one tried to influence them.

In less than an hour the jury returned and the foreman announced their findings: "Guilty on all counts."

The defendants paled. Haines shook his head in disbelief, and the judge looked pleased.

Evans briefly opened his coat enabling Jimmy to see the Colt in his belt, but there was no sign of any disturbance about to break out. Judge Bennett adjourned the court, saying, "I will do the sentencing first thing in the morning."

Jimmy hurried to the Savoy and wired the paper the following:

> To Ed Harris, Austin American Statesman, Austin, Texas
>
> All defendants found guilty on all counts. There was no outbreak of violence that had been predicted. Judge Bennett will pronounce sentence tomorrow morning. Will report again tomorrow after sentencing.
> Jimmy Dickens
LTC

After he finished sending the wire, he had another bourbon and ate a sandwich in the coffee shop. Then he picked up a letter from Colleen at the front desk and went to the room to read it.

> My Dearest Jimmy,
>
> I am missing you so much; sometimes I miss you and worry about you so much I have trouble sleeping at night. I think if I didn't have this job I would go completely crazy.
>
> I love my job working for Mr. McGill; he is so nice to me and only yells at me once in a while.
>
> At night I try to stay busy making plans for our wedding. I will tell you all about them when you come home.
>
> Please stay safe and hurry home. I love you so much.
> --Colleen

Jimmy read the letter twice, then folded it and tucked it into his shirt pocket.

The next morning Evans came by the Savoy to have breakfast as they had prearranged the day before. While Jimmy had flapjacks and bacon, Evans had only one biscuit.

Evans told him, "I don't know how you stay so skinny, eating as much as you do."

"Maybe it's because I am ten years younger than you. It will probably catch up with me some day, but I am going to enjoy it while I can," Jimmy replied.

As they walked to the courthouse together, Evans said, "Well, one more day to worry then we can quit worrying. When you give me your Colt, I'll stick it in my belt. So stay close to me so I can hand it to you if there is any trouble."

"That's a deal, but I hope there won't be any trouble. I have a great little lady I intend to marry as soon as I get back home," Jimmy told him.

As soon as they took their seats, two uniformed deputies brought the defendants into the room, the judge gaveled the court into session, and the sentencing part of the trial began.

In very short order the judge sentenced all of the three defendants to ten years at hard labor and Clark to be tried later for the multiple murders he committed.

Jimmy noticed three men enter the courtroom and stand in the back observing the proceedings. He saw that the men were all wearing tan-colored full-length dusters, but that was normal dress for anyone making a long journey on horseback. It kept the dust from getting on their clothing. Evans also noticed the intruders and inched his way closer to Jimmy.

Within seconds all hell broke loose. One of the men took out a 12-gauge double-barrel shotgun and emptied both barrels at Judge Bennett. Evans tossed Jimmy's pistol to him, then fired his pistol, killing the man with the shotgun. Then the other men drew pistols and opened fire at the two deputies guarding Clark. One of them was killed and the other wounded. The judge, though wounded, took a pistol from under his robe and fired at the intruders as did Jimmy.

Then Clark bolted for the door, but Evans shot him in the leg, causing him to tumble to the floor. Then the assailants were assaulted and killed by a volley of gunfire from Evans, Jimmy, and the judge. When the smoke cleared, all three assailants were dead, as was one of the deputies, and one juror. The wounded included Judge Bennett, one deputy, one juror, and Clark, who rolled on the floor writhing in agony.

Jimmy helped Evans load the wounded into a wagon, and then raced to the telegraph office to send a wire to the paper, as Evans drove the wagon to the hospital. They agreed to meet later at the bar in the Savoy.

He was completely out of breath by the time he reached the telegraph office, but he sat down and composed the following wire:

> To Ed Harris, Austin American Statesman, Austin, Texas
>
> This morning after Judge Bennett sentenced all defendants to ten years at hard labor and Clark to stand trial later for multiple murders, violence erupted in courtroom. Three men in dusters arrived and started shooting at the judge, deputy guards, and the jury. They were eventually killed by shots from Judge Bennett, the bailiff Evans, one deputy, and this reporter. Wounded were Judge Bennett, one juror, one deputy, and Clark, who was shot while trying to escape. The wounded were taken to a hospital.
>
> Will wire later with report on their condition.
>
>   --Jimmy Dickens
>   LTC

Then Jimmy walked to the Savoy bar and downed one quick bourbon, then ordered another one to sip as he waited for Evans to join him. As he waited he thought, *Damn, this job is dangerous, just like Harris warned me it would be. I have been lucky so far, and I hope my luck will hold up.*

Before Jimmy had finished his second bourbon, Emmett sat down next to him at the bar.

Jimmy anxiously asked him "How is the judge?"

"Well, he will live, but he has lost sight in one eye. The dumb bastard who shot him loaded his shotgun with birdshot. If he had loaded it with buck shot, the judge would be dead," was the answer. "The deputy was badly wounded, but the doctors think he will live and that damned Clark will survive the shot I put into his leg."

"I'm sure glad Judge Bennett survived the assault," Jimmy offered.

Then Evans continued, "I think I have the whole thing figured out now. Those three shooters are the same ones who wounded the guards, took the wagon, and hid it. Clark knew who they were all along, got word to them, and wanted them to bust him out before he had to stand trial for the multiple murders. He didn't give a damn what happened to the other guys on trial; he only cared about himself."

Jimmy agreed by saying, "I'll bet you're exactly right. That all makes sense. Now the only thing left is Clark's trial, and it will all be over and I can get home."

"Yes, and you can bet if Judge Bennett is well enough to preside at his trial, his ass will hang. The judge is really pissed off at losing his eye." The two of them had one more drink together. Then Evans left for home and Jimmy went to his room, totally exhausted from the eventful day.

He was still groggy when he was awakened by loud knocking on his door and shouts of "Jimmy, Jimmy, wake up! Something important has happened!" It was Evans.

Jimmy stumbled to the door and grumbled "What in the hell would be important enough to wake me up at this time of night after the day we both had yesterday?"

Evans explained, "Clark is dead. There was a guard posted in the hall outside his door, but someone climbed up the fire escape went through the window, covered his head with a pillow, and stabbed him to death. The guard didn't hear a thing."

Jimmy answered, "Good. I'm glad the son of a bitch is dead. Does anyone know who did it?"

"No, and they will probably never know. I suspect it was probably done by one of his co-defendants he was throwing to the wolves," Evans said.

Jimmy hurriedly dressed, and he and Evans went down to the coffee shop and ate breakfast, discussing the case the entire time they ate.

They parted after they ate, Evans explaining he had not yet been to bed, planned to sleep all day, but agreed to meet Jimmy for dinner that evening.

Jimmy adjourned to his room and wrote this wire to the paper.

> To Ed Harris, Austin American Statesman, Austin, Texas:
> Learned late last night Clark was stabbed to death in his hospital room, despite guard in the hall outside his door. Believe assassin gained access through window. Judge Bennett will recover but lost sight in one eye. Wounded deputy will recover. Assignment is over so I plan on taking tomorrow's train to San Antonio, then stage to Austin day after tomorrow, unless you have further assignment.
> --Jimmy Dickens
> LTC

The exhausted Jimmy lay down on the bed, fully dressed and awaiting an answer to the wire he sent. He slept until a bellboy rapped on his door with a reply from Harris.

> To Jimmy Dickens, Savoy Hotel, Houston, Texas
> Great job as usual. Putting out EXTRA paper today. No further assignment. Come home.
> --Ed Harris

Jimmy read the wire, breathed a sigh of relief, and went back to sleep.

That evening Jimmy and Emmett had dinner together. Jimmy told him, "I want to thank you for your help, and my paper also thanks you for the help you gave me. I will consider you friend forever."

"I feel the same about you, and I hope we can stay in touch," Evans replied.

After dinner they gave each other a hearty handshake, and Jimmy spent the evening packing, excited by the prospect of being home and safe with Colleen again.

The next morning he checked out of the hotel, signed for the charges, which looked to him like the national debt, and left for the train depot. That evening he checked into the Menger Hotel. He slept well. The next morning he boarded the stage for Austin. Colleen met him at the stagecoach stop and told him they both had two days off.

She had bought a bottle of champagne, and they planned on finishing the bottle before going to bed to get acquainted all over again. He had been gone for three months, and for two people in love, that seemed a lifetime.

It was then that Colleen dropped a bombshell on him saying, "Jimmy, have you noticed I haven't mentioned my throbbing any more?"

"I'm afraid I have been too busy to notice," he replied.

"Well, you had better start paying more attention to me. I am going to have our baby. I was so afraid something would happen to you and our baby wouldn't have a daddy," she said.

He held her close and told her, "Please don't worry. I am going to be around for a long time, and I'll be a good daddy for the baby. If it's a boy, I'm going to name him Billy."

"That is a great idea," she agreed, and kissed him.

After two days of love making and planning their wedding, it was time for both of them to return to work. When they arrived at the paper, Colleen left him behind and went to her desk outside McGill's office. She did not want to detract from the welcome Harris had prepared for him. Handshakes, hugs, pats on the back, and congratulations were heaped on him. Jimmy was slightly embarrassed by the accolades.

Then Harris explained, "Your story on Clark's murder and the conclusion of the trial scooped everyone. We have been deluged with wires from all of the other Texas papers asking for details and for permission to reprint your article. Of course we will furnish it, but it is going to cost them. How in the hell did you find all of that out?"

"I had a friend," Jimmy explained.

"Well, you have a pretty substantial bonus coming for that story, so you might want to buy your friend a present."

"I will," Jimmy answered.

After work Jimmy and Colleen went to dinner at the Press Club, toasted each other with champagne, ate a steak dinner, then went home to work on wedding plans.

Jimmy deferred to Colleen's wishes, but both agreed there would be too many people to have the wedding at the Baptist Church in New Braunfels. They finally agreed to have the wedding at the Press Club in Austin, and the wedding reception there after the wedding. They both agreed, however, that a lot of New Braunfels people would be invited, including Colleen's family and Miss Braun. Jimmy promised to take care of the arrangements if Colleen would handle the guest list and the mailing of the invitations.

Chapter 22

JIMMY AND COLLEEN ARE MARRIED

The Press Club was the only ballroom large enough to accommodate the large crowd that was expected, so in an unorthodox way it was decided to have the guests seated at the dining tables, and they would remain seated while the wedding was taking place at the front of the room. Two tables were taken up by the bosses and co-workers of the bride and groom; one table was occupied by Colleen's family and Miss Braun; and another table had the guests invited from Port Arthur and Houston.

Ed Harris had agreed to be Jimmy's best man, and Colleen's father would give her away. Her sister would be maid of honor.

Emmett Evans was almost late for the ceremony but arrived early enough for Jimmy to give him a silver plated Remington Derringer, telling him it was thanks for helping get the story that scooped all of the other papers and earned him a hefty bonus.

The Methodist minister conducted a short but beautiful service. Jimmy put the ring on Colleen's finger, kissed her, and at last they were married.

The partying began instantly. There were two bars, and they were constantly crowded.

Dinner was served early at Colleen's request, but some people kept drinking during dinner.

With the crowd distracted by the revelry, Jimmy and Colleen were able to slip out and make their way to a secret destination for a short honeymoon.

The following year was a busy one for the newlyweds. Colleen quit her job at the paper and stayed home to care for their new baby, Billy.

Jimmy immersed himself in his new job as a crime reporter. There was more than enough crime to keep him busy. The returning Civil War veterans, unable to find honest jobs, turned to robbing banks, trains, and stagecoaches. This sudden outburst of crime caused the governor to reestablish the Texas Rangers. The Rangers were veterans themselves of the war and set up their headquarters in Garland with frontier regiments in San Antonio, Austin, and Houston.

When he was not working, Jimmy enjoyed his new life with Colleen and his new son, Billy.

He did find time to start a book about his adventures during the war. He planned on calling it *Two Brothers: A Story of the Civil War and Brotherly Love*.